Also by Sherryl Woods

Hide and Seek
Bank on It
Stolen Moments
Body and Soul
Reckless
Ties That Bind

Published by
WARNER BOOKS

Sherryl Woods

Wages of Sin

WARNER BOOKS

A Time Warner Company

Enjoy lively book discussions online with CompuServe. To become a
member of CompuServe call 1-800-848-8199 and ask for the Time
Warner Trade Publishing forum. (Current members GO:TWEP.)

WARNER BOOKS EDITION

Cover design by Jackie Merri Meyer
Cover photo by Herman Estevez
Hand lettering by Carl Dellacroce

Warner Books, Inc.
1271 Avenue of the Americas
New York, NY 10020

 A Time Warner Company

Printed in the United States of America

First Printing: October, 1994

10 9 8 7 6 5 4 3 2 1

NOR

CHAPTER

One

*T*HE suicide of Mary Allison Watkins bumped world politics, the Braves' Pennant race, and a local business scandal right off the front page of Atlanta's papers. For two days the headlines were as tawdry as any tabloid's in America. They were fueled by speculation about why a beautiful, successful assistant to Georgia's senior senator would suddenly decide to drive her brand-new Jaguar straight into a two-hundred-year-old oak tree at a speed sufficient to jam the front bumper all the way to the tailpipe.

Joe Donelli waved the most gruesome of the front-page photos under his new wife's nose. "Let this be a lesson to you, Amanda," he said. "The way you drive, you're destined to wind up wrapped around a tree just like this one day."

Amanda shoved aside the newspaper. "It was a clear day," she informed him. "She was out in the country, for

1

heaven's sakes. Traffic was light. According to authorities, no one had tampered with any part of the car. There was no evidence she ever hit the brakes. There was no medical reason, no sign of a stroke or a seizure or a heart attack, no alcohol or drugs in her bloodstream.''

She drew in a deep breath for her summation. ''Therefore—and I have this on the best law enforcement and medical authority willing to be quoted by the media—Mary Allison Watkins aimed at that tree. It was a suicide, Donelli. Not an accident. It's not the least bit relevant to the way I drive.''

''Maybe not directly relevant,'' he conceded grudgingly. ''But every time you squeal out of the driveway, an image just like this one forms in my mind. Call me overly protective, but I'd really like this marriage of ours to last at least long enough to celebrate our first anniversary. We have ten months to go.''

Amanda refused to be drawn into a lengthy discussion of her driving skills. If Donelli had expected a wedding ceremony, especially one that had lasted ten minutes and been witnessed by six people, to change all of her bad habits, they were in for a long period of adjustment. She was having enough trouble remembering to put the cap back onto the toothpaste. Given their disagreements over that, a conversation about her driving could send them straight to divorce court.

''Why do you suppose she did it?'' she asked, hoping to send his too vivid imagination off in another, more productive direction.

Donelli had once been a crackerjack homicide detective in a tough jurisdiction—Brooklyn. He now dabbled in private investigations, when he wasn't tending to his fields of corn, Vidalia onions, and tomatoes. No one she knew was better at devising theories and assembling the evidence to back them up. That was precisely why she wanted him focusing on Mary Allison Watkins's motivations and not what he perceived as Amanda's own dangerous driving skills. Given a little time, he was sure to come up with a couple of convincing arguments to go along with that sickening newspaper photo. Then he'd have her driving twenty miles an hour under the limit like some timid little old lady.

She met his gaze across the breakfast table. She still wasn't quite used to facing all that brawn and intelligence over cornflakes, although she admitted she rather liked seeing him every day after all. She figured that was a good sign. Given the rocky road of their courtship and her own marital track record, she hadn't been convinced she'd make it past the second week.

"Why would a woman who had it all kill herself?" she mused aloud, casting a sly look in Donelli's direction. He didn't seem to be jumping at the bait. In fact, he shrugged with seeming indifference. Apparently he'd found something more interesting to read, probably a weather report.

"Come on, Joe, think about it. This is your area of expertise."

He did glance up at the hint of flattery, though his

expression was faintly bewildered. "How did you come up with that idea?"

"You can't solve murders as well as you did without being good at deducing motives. So why'd she do it?"

"Obviously her life wasn't as rosy as it appeared on the surface," he said, and went back to whatever he was reading.

Amanda wasn't about to let it rest at that. She could have figured out that much on her own. "According to the paper, she whizzed through college on an academic scholarship and never slowed down. She had a responsible position with a powerful senator. She was intelligent and gorgeous. She was engaged to be married to Representative Zachary Downs, one of the most eligible bachelors on Capitol Hill and a rising star in the House." Amanda shook her head. "I just don't get it."

"Maybe she and Downs were having problems," he muttered from behind the sports section.

She waved off the possibility. "Have you seen the interviews he's done? The man is devastated."

With a sigh of resignation, Donelli folded the paper and put it aside. "Amanda, would you really expect him to be doing cartwheels down Pennsylvania Avenue? If they were having problems, it's hardly something he'd be inclined to reveal under these circumstances. He'd keep it private."

"So you buy the suicide theory?"

"I haven't seen any evidence to the contrary," he responded cautiously as if he sensed that it was a trick question.

"Then how come no one has found a note?" she demanded, seizing on what she saw as a significant flaw in his argument, and everyone else's, for that matter.

"Why hasn't one single person come forward to talk about how depressed she was over something, *anything?*" she added. "To hear her friends talk about her, Mary Allison was more upbeat than one of those disgustingly cheery morning talk show hostesses. It was one of the traits that made her so successful in Washington. Nothing rattled her."

Donelli looked bemused. "Not five minutes ago you were telling me it was suicide. You laid out all the evidence, detail by detail. Let me guess. At that moment, it was a convenient explanation. Now you have another agenda."

"Not exactly. I'm just puzzled," she said as an idea began to take shape for an article for *Inside Atlanta*, where she specialized in investigative journalism. It wasn't a career that policemen in general and Donelli in particular found particularly noble.

"Did you see anything in the paper about the funeral?" she asked.

"If I had, I'm not so sure I'd tell you. Don't you think there's something a little bizarre about going to a stranger's funeral just to satisfy some morbid curiosity?"

"Morbid curiosity?" she repeated with what she hoped was convincing indignation. "I'm a reporter. I'm paid to be curious about things that don't add up. There's nothing morbid about it. Besides, who said anything about going?"

"I know you. I also know that you are a magazine reporter who is not assigned to do a story on Mary Allison Watkins. In my book, if you turn up at that church, that makes you no better than the voyeurs who watch those tabloid exposés on television."

Amanda ignored his disdain. She was more interested in his unconscious slip. "It was in the paper, then."

"I never said that."

"You mentioned *that church* as if you'd read about where the service was going to be."

He shook his head. "Am I going to have to watch every single word I utter around you?"

"For all the days of your life," she assured him, reaching for the paper. That exasperating prospect ought to keep him from worrying excessively about whether she was off attending the funeral of a total stranger.

An hour later, however, she was careful to make the turn from the driveway onto the highway without her car's tires squealing. It was important that Donelli see that she could make some compromises in the name of marital harmony.

There were so many carnations, roses, gladioli, and other more exotic flowers at the front of the stately old Episcopal church that the air reeked with their heavy, sweet scent. With the pews filled to capacity and the overflow crowd jammed along the aisles, it was all Amanda could do to breathe.

Considering Donelli's low opinion of her presence at

the funeral, she'd expected to feel like some sneaky tabloid reporter. Instead she was too busy trying to stir up a breeze with the little cardboard fan decorated with a picture of Jesus. His arms were held wide in a welcoming gesture that relieved some of her guilt over being at the service.

"We are here today to mourn the loss of Mary Allison Watkins and to commend her soul to eternal peace," the minister intoned from the front of the church.

The mourners fell silent. Only a feminine sob, quickly muted, spoiled the solemn hush as the Reverend John Lawton repeated the Twenty-third Psalm. "The Lord is my Shepherd . . ."

Amanda let the soothing prayer flow over her as she surveyed the crowd. She spotted what had to be Mary Allison's family in the first pew—two women and a man. She couldn't guess the relationships, though there was a bit of a family resemblance between one of the women and the man. That same woman was flanked by Representative Zachary Downs and Senator Blaine Rawlings.

Even from a distance, the 37-year-old Downs looked dry-eyed and stoic, his complexion ashen. Not once did his glance stray to the black-and-gold casket with its lavish blanket of white roses.

The distinguished, white-haired senator had a supportive arm around the woman who, Amanda decided, must be Mary Allison's mother. She was obviously the source of those echoing sobs. Her thin shoulders shook with them. Periodically the senator bent close and murmured something, then offered her a pristine handkerchief, which she declined with a curt shake of her head. There was an anger to the gesture that was an odd counterpoint to the senator's seeming solicitousness.

Amanda wasn't sure what she'd expected to discover at the service, but she walked away from the church in the pouring rain an hour later still feeling strangely disconcerted. The eulogies had been heartfelt and touching. The traditional hymns had been moving. But like Mrs. Watkins's annoyance, something had been out of sync about the whole ceremony. She toyed with the possibilities all the way to the *Inside Atlanta* offices but couldn't put her finger on it.

It was past noon when she finally got to her desk, still puzzling over why Mary Allison's suicide bothered her so. Given the powerful people involved, the police investigation had been rapid and thorough. Publicly, at least, there hadn't been the faintest hint of doubt about the ruling that the young woman had taken her own life.

Yet try as she might, Amanda couldn't come up with a plausible explanation for a woman who'd shown absolutely no evidence of being distraught to willfully slam her car into a tree on a virtually deserted Georgia backroad. If someone was determined to die, there were more certain ways to go about it. Hitting a tree could just as easily have left her maimed rather than dead.

Grabbing up a handful of tangerine jelly beans, Amanda wandered into the executive editor's office. Sometimes just sparring with Oscar Cates helped her to pin down her chaotic thoughts. His tendency to take the official stance allowed her to give full rein to her love of playing devil's advocate.

She noticed right off that Oscar was looking even more slovenly than usual this morning. He'd apparently dressed in whatever had tumbled out of the dryer, a mussed pin-striped shirt, wash-and-wear khaki pants and a tie that could have used a trip to the dry cleaner. He could spruce up amazingly well for special occasions, but work wasn't one of them, especially with his watchdog wife out of town on a New York shopping spree with her friends. She usually sent him out looking presentable, at least.

Oscar glanced up from his computer, glared at Amanda over his hated reading glasses, and waved her toward a chair. "In a minute," he muttered.

Amanda wasn't terrific at waiting. She paced.

Apparently distracted by her movements, he looked up and scowled. "I thought I told you to sit."

"I wasn't aware it was an order," she said, and dutifully sat. She figured she had to at least start their conversation with a cooperative attitude if she hoped to get him to go along with her still somewhat vague story idea. She gestured toward the computer. "Go on and finish. I'll wait."

He regarded her suspiciously. Obviously she'd over-done being agreeable.

"What are you after, Amanda?"

"I wanted to discuss a feature for the next issue with you."

"A feature?" he repeated doubtfully. "I thought you considered all features to be fluff, a waste of trees, et cetera, et cetera, ad nauseam."

He was right. Generally she did think features lacked substance, but then she and Oscar had rather divergent opinions about what constituted a feature. He wanted fluff about historic home tours and quilting circles. She wanted to do an in-depth profile of an apparently happy, successful woman who'd committed suicide. At least she thought that was the angle.

"Maybe I used the wrong term," she said. "I've spent the whole morning thinking about Mary Allison Watkins. I think there's a story there. What would make a woman like her kill herself? I could even talk to some experts about depression, signs of suicidal tendencies."

She added the coup de grace, which was bound to appeal to Oscar's image of *Inside Atlanta*'s noble role in the community. "It would be a real public service piece, especially in these stressful times," she said.

His expression brightened, just as she'd expected. "Public service, huh? I like that. I'm glad you're finally thinking of all the good we can do, Amanda. It's our duty to make a contribution to the way of life in this town. Not every story has to be a major exposé."

Amanda couldn't argue with his good intentions, even though her personal approach to journalism tended toward shining glaring light into shadowy corners. As far as she was concerned, that did more public good than all the cheerful features about annual parades, dogwood festivals, and historic restoration projects combined.

"So it's okay for me to go ahead with this?" she said. "I can put everything else on the back burner?"

His gaze narrowed. "You'll still give me some copy on the wives of the Atlanta Braves players, right?"

Amanda figured it would require about ten minutes to dash off the sort of puff piece he was looking for to go with the photo spread for the October issue. How hard could it be to sum up the wives' view of World Series mania? She could already guess how impossible their husbands were to live with as baseball season came down to the wire. Personally she couldn't imagine anything more boring to write or to read. Still, she managed to inject the expected note of enthusiasm into her voice. "Absolutely."

"You figure you'll have this suicide thing for the next issue, too?"

She nodded. "Can you hold back maybe four pages in the middle, plus room for a jump?"

"In other words, you want the cover," he said with a sigh of resignation. "Damn it, Amanda, you were at the news meeting. You know I've already got a big business story in that space. Jack Davis has been pulling it together for the past month. What am I supposed to tell him?"

She resisted pointing out that that was his problem as editor. "Give me twenty-four hours on this before you finalize the cover. If I come up with something really solid, we'll negotiate."

He looked as if he wanted to refuse just on principle, but it wasn't in Oscar's nature to turn his back on the possibility of a story that would undoubtedly boost circulation. Mary Allison had been viewed as a heroine in Atlanta, a local girl who'd stormed Washington and brought it to heel. Her suicide was good copy. If a scandal was attached, so much the better.

"You think there's something more to this, don't you?" he inquired hopefully.

"Oscar, I don't know what to think," she said honestly.

"Twenty-four hours, then. Not a minute more. Agreed?"

She glanced at her watch pointedly. "Twelve forty-six Wednesday. I swear it."

Back at her desk, she jotted down a list of prospective sources, beginning with Mrs. Watkins, Representative Downs, Senator Rawlings, and the senator's chief of staff, Gregory Fine, a weasely little man with whom Amanda had already had one too many run-ins. No doubt there were other friends and relatives who could give her insight into Mary Allison's state of mind in the days before her death. She'd get to them later.

With no time to waste, she cast aside her distaste for intruding on a private moment of grief and called the Watkins house.

"Mrs. Watkins is in no condition to speak to the media," the man who answered told Amanda in a tone that managed to straddle the fence between southern charm and outright rudeness. "I'm sure you understand."

Whether she did or she didn't apparently didn't matter. He hung up on her.

She could have called back and hoped for a more cooperative family friend or relative, but something about the man's tone suggested that there wasn't a chance in hell that a reporter was going to be allowed to speak to the bereaved mother. It was exactly the kind of attitude that stirred Amanda's journalistic suspicions. Anyone who knew her could have told the man that warning her away would only strengthen her determination. She'd just have to go out there, preferably after everyone had left.

In the meantime she called her favorite homicide detective, Jim Harrison, the only man she knew who was perpetually more rumpled than Oscar.

"Gee, it's been weeks. To what do I owe this honor?" he inquired. "I didn't think you were chasing knifings in the ghetto and drive-by shootings yet. That's all I've got on my desk."

"Maybe there's something that ought to be there," she suggested casually.

"You know about a body stashed somewhere?"

He sounded more amused than fascinated. Amanda decided to up the stakes. "Actually the body's buried, but I think the clues are elsewhere," she said. She could practically hear his mind clicking.

"Stop with the riddles, Amanda," he said finally. "Just spit it out."

"I was just wondering how closely the police checked Mary Allison Watkins's car."

"I read the same papers you do. The experts went over that car with a fine-tooth comb."

"Looking for?"

"Mechanical malfunctions."

"What about paint from another car?"

Dead silence greeted the suggestion.

"Oh, Detective, are you there?"

"I'm here."

"Well?"

"You know it's not my case," he said predictably.

"But I do know you love to dabble in things mysterious. How about checking with the technicians who went over that car? Maybe you can find out where it's stashed so I can go take a look at it myself?"

"You're opening a real can of worms here, you know that, don't you?"

"Not unless somebody's covering something up," she reminded him. "If everything's just as it's supposed to be, I'll have nothing to report, will I?"

He sighed heavily, something the men she knew tended to do a lot.

"You know I trust your instincts, but just this once I hope there was a major glitch with your reception," he said.

"You'll check, though, won't you?"

"I'll check. I'll get back to you when I know anything."

Amanda read through the computer files on the accident one more time. By then it was nearly rush hour. She left the office and drove to the neighborhood of aging middle-class homes where Dee-Ann Watkins had raised her super-achiever daughter. There were still a dozen or more cars in the driveway and lining the shaded street in front of the small brick ranch-style house. Amanda parked down the block and settled back to watch.

At seven o'clock the last of the mourners began to straggle out. A limo turned the corner, then double-parked in front until Zachary Downs emerged from the house. He lingered on the front steps for a few final moments with Mrs. Watkins. Whatever he was saying did not seem to be consoling her. She looked every bit as angry as she had for that one fleeting second back at the church.

As he walked to the limo, he was joined by a young woman who had exited the house right after him. She had a classic blond beauty, enhanced by her understated but obviously expensive black suit. Even though it was dusk, she work dark sunglasses. Amanda tried to read Zack Downs's expression as he helped the woman into the limo, but it was enigmatic. There was no way she could guess the exact nature of the relationship.

After the pair had left, only two cars remained in the driveway. Amanda assumed that one of them belonged to Mrs. Watkins. She debated waiting for the owner of the second car to leave, then decided that more than likely whoever remained was a relative or friend staying on at the house. With less than a day left to convince Oscar that she had a cover story for the next edition of *Inside Atlanta*, she didn't have time to waste.

She rang the bell, then waited, rehearsing the speech she hoped would get her inside.

After a lengthy delay, Mrs. Watkins opened the door. Her narrow face was pale, her eyes red-rimmed, but the look she directed at Amanda was more weary than confrontative.

Amanda introduced herself. "I'm terribly sorry to bother you at a time like this."

Dee-Ann Watkins studied her suspiciously. "You another reporter? I've already told the rest of 'em I got nothing to say."

"I'm with *Inside Atlanta*. I really would like to speak to you about Mary Allison's death. I promise I won't take up much of your time."

Dark brown eyes clashed with hers. "How come you didn't call it a suicide like everybody else?"

Simple courtesy had kept her from using the word, but Amanda sensed something in Mrs. Watkins's reaction that kept her from admitting that. "There are a few things about that that puzzle me," she said instead.

"Is that so?" Mrs. Watkins said. "Well, to tell you the truth, I'm puzzled by it, too."

"Couldn't we talk, then? Perhaps we can clarify a few things," Amanda said, sensing that Mrs. Watkins was just itching to set the record straight. She added what she hoped would be the convincing argument. "I want people to know what Mary Allison was really like."

Mrs. Watkins gave a curt, approving nod at that and stood aside to let Amanda enter. "I'll tell you about my girl all right. And I'll tell you why I know with every bone in my body that Mary Allison didn't kill herself. She just wouldn't have done it, especially not now."

CHAPTER

Two

A SAD collection of family photo albums, high
school and college yearbooks, and newspaper clip-
pings littered the coffee table in Mrs. Watkins's
otherwise tidy living room. There wasn't a speck of dust
on the scarred furniture, which looked as if it might have
been assembled from secondhand stores back in the sixties.
It was a hodgepodge of Danish modern and dark, heavy
Spanish. A stand filled with extraordinarily healthy ferns
and African violets sat under the window. Amanda killed
such potted plants simply by bringing them into her house.
Maybe living with a farmer would improve her luck.

"How about a cup of coffee? Maybe some coconut
cake?" Dee Ann Watkins urged as if she were used to
bustling around and waiting on people. There were a few
strands of gray in her short dark hair and most likely
temporary lines of exhaustion on her face. Otherwise she
looked no more than forty, though Amanda guessed she

probably had to be closer to fifty, depending on how old she'd been when Mary Allison was born.

"There's no need for you to go to any trouble," Amanda told her.

"It's no trouble." She gestured toward a dining room table still laden with casseroles and trays of desserts. "Somebody has to eat all this food. I can't imagine what people think I'm going to do with it all by myself. There's enough to feed the entire neighborhood for a month." She sighed. "I suppose people don't know what else to do."

"I'm sure that's it," Amanda agreed, surreptitiously glancing around to see if she could discover who owned that second car in the driveway. Unfortunately not another soul was in sight, and there were no sounds from other parts of the house. She finally gave up and tried a more direct route. "I'm sure it'll help with your guests, though."

"Guests?" Mrs. Watkins repeated, looking confused. "There's no one here but me."

"I just assumed . . . I mean, there is a second car in the driveway."

"Oh, that. That was Mary Allison's, before she got the Jaguar. She kept it here for times when she came to town. This time, because of the wedding coming up and all, she brought that fancy new car with her. Wanted me to see it. It was her wedding present from Zack. Did you know that?"

"No, I didn't," she said, wondering how he felt knowing that his gift had played such an important part in her tragic death. She started to follow Mrs. Watkins into the kitchen. "May I help with the coffee?"

"No indeed," Mrs. Watkins told her. "Does me good to keep busy. You go on and look at those pictures and things. You'll see what I mean about Mary Allison. She wasn't the kind of girl to run away from her problems by killing herself."

The last was said adamantly. Mrs. Watkins, despite the stress of the day's funeral, was not hysterical. Nor did she sound as if she were in denial. She sounded downright furious that anyone would think ill of her child and dead set on wanting to prove that the authorities were blinded to the truth. It was Amanda's good fortune and persistence that had made her the beneficiary of Mrs. Watkins's need to unburden herself.

While she waited for the cake and coffee, Amanda turned the pages of the family album. The pretty brunette child with the huge brown eyes so much like her mother's was on every page, from toothless baby pictures to smiling snapshots taken at college graduation. Dee-Ann was with her in some of the photos, but there was no sign of Mr. Watkins, not even in the earliest pictures. If Mrs. Watkins had been a struggling single mother, no wonder she was so proud of her daughter's extraordinary achievements.

When Mrs. Watkins returned, she handed Amanda a thick slice of the homemade cake with its moist flakes of fresh coconut coating the layer of creamy frosting.

"Try it," she urged. "My sister-in-law bakes the best in town. I can't tell you how many prizes she's won, though why anyone would want to spend their time entering bake-offs is beyond me.''

Amanda dutifully sampled the cake under her hostess's watchful eye. The speed with which she finished the entire piece had little to do with her desire to get on with her interview. As promised, it was delicious. She told Mrs. Watkins exactly that.

"I'm glad you liked it. I'll be sure and tell Ruthie. She just loves knowing she has another conquest." She picked up an album, the one with all the baby pictures, and stroked the leather binding. "Did you look through this?"

Amanda nodded. "She was a beautiful child."

"She was, wasn't she?" she said, her eyes brimming with unshed tears. "She never gave me a bit of trouble. It wasn't always easy, believe you me. There were just the two of us. Her father was killed in a car accident while I was carrying Mary Allison. She never knew her daddy."

She brushed at her tears, then regarded Amanda intently. "That's why I know this wasn't any accident and it wasn't any suicide. Mary Allison knew how I felt about fast driving and such. She was always careful behind the wheel, always maintained her car in top condition. And of all the ways in the world she might have chosen to kill herself, it wouldn't have been this way, not knowing what it would do to me to be reminded of how her daddy died."

Amanda agreed. "Did you tell the police that?"

"Spelled it out in plain English, but they liked their tidy little solution much better."

"Did they have some evidence proving it was suicide?

A note, maybe? Had she been distraught about something lately?''

"There was no note, because it wasn't a suicide," she insisted vehemently.

Her look dared Amanda to contradict her. Amanda wisely remained silent. Apparently satisfied, Mrs. Watkins went on.

"Besides, she was busy planning a wedding. The very day she died she and I had been to look at wedding dresses at Neiman-Marcus. She put a hundred-dollar deposit down on one. Does that sound like something a woman would do if she planned on dying that very afternoon?" she scoffed as she carefully put the album aside with one last caress.

"No," Amanda said. "But it might have been a simple accident."

Mrs. Watkins shot her a disbelieving glare. "I went out there and looked for myself. That road was straight as a yardstick. There wasn't a drop of rain or an oil slick that might have sent her car out of control."

"So what do you think happened?"

"I think somebody ran her off that road. Maybe they chased her, scared the daylights out of her, then tapped a fender and sent the car into that tree."

It was a scenario that made too much sense to Amanda. That's why she'd asked Jim Harrison about the car's paint just that morning. Right now, though, she was intent on playing devil's advocate to keep Dee-Ann Watkins talking. "But the police . . ."

Mrs. Watkins snorted. "With Zack Downs and Blaine Rawlings breathing down their necks, exactly how much effort do you suppose the sheriff out there or the police here in town put into checking out what really happened?"

"But why would Mary Allison's fiancé and her boss want her murder covered up?"

"Why indeed," the woman said mysteriously.

This was no time for Dee-Ann Watkins to turn enigmatic. "Is there something you're not telling me?" Amanda demanded, fighting hard not to lose patience and blow the fragile rapport she had established with the woman. "Did Mary Allison know something she wasn't supposed to know? Was she a threat to them in some way? Do you think somebody lured her out there that afternoon?"

Mrs. Watkins's shoulders sagged. Fresh tears welled up in her eyes, but she brushed them away as if she were exasperated at the show of emotion. "That's what I don't know. She never talked much to me about work. I did have the feeling she was worrying about something when she came home this last weekend. It was like something heavy was weighing on her mind. I thought that was why she went for a drive, to think things through."

"You mean she was depressed?"

"No, absolutely not. It was more like she had a decision that had to be made and she didn't want to make it. There was always a lot of pressure in a job like hers, but usually she thrived on it."

"Is there anyone she might have talked it over with?

Anyone she would have confided in? Her fiancé, perhaps? A girlfriend?''

Mrs. Watkins shook her head. ''Mary Allison wasn't the sort to put her problems off on somebody else. I'm not real sure that Zack's the kind of man a woman could confide in anyway, if you know what I mean. He's a little stiff and formal for my taste, but Mary Allison adored him, and I have to say he was good to her.''

''There are no brothers or sisters?''

''No. She was an only child. I never remarried. It made her something of a loner, I suppose. That was the bad side. The good side was that it gave her a sense of independence, the kind of quiet strength that serves a woman well.''

Amanda tried to figure out whom such a woman would trust. ''Who were her bridesmaids?''

''She just planned on two attendants. Her maid of honor was supposed to be Valerie LaPalma. She works in the senator's office and was here today, but she's gone back up to Washington.''

Amanda recalled the woman she'd seen leaving with Downs and made a guess. ''She's petite, blond. She was wearing a gorgeous black suit.''

''You saw her?''

''She left with Zack Downs.''

''Yes. That's Valerie.''

She said it without any hint that she was suspicious of the coziness between Zack and the maid of honor. Amanda didn't want to start that kind of speculation, at least not yet.

She just filed the information away. "And Mary Allison's bridesmaid?"

"Her bridesmaid was Lou-Ellen Kinsale. Mary Allison and Lou-Ellen went all through school together. She still lives here in Atlanta. She works out at the mall, in one of the record shops, maybe. She always did have a fondness for music. She was going to sing at the wedding, in fact."

It sounded as if Lou-Ellen would be the most accessible of the prospective sources. Amanda got addresses and phone numbers for as many people as she thought she might need, then thanked Mrs. Watkins.

"You find out who killed my girl. That's all I want," she said. "Then I want to be there to see that they rot in hell."

Somewhere between the Watkins house and the mall, Amanda remembered that she had a husband waiting for her at home. She was two hours later than she'd anticipated being. Donelli was going to be bouncing off walls. Although he'd promised never to object to her working whatever hours she needed to, he did expect a little common courtesy in return. Like a phone call.

She punched in the number on her car phone and anticipated the explosion likely on the other end of the line.

"Where are you?" Joe inquired.

His tone was deceptively mild. Amanda wasn't fooled. He was borderline livid and trying to hide it. "On the road," she answered. "I'm heading over to the mall to try to track down a source. I'll be home right after. I could pick up dinner on the way.''

"Dinner is on the table. Pete has already eaten. He suggested we send out a search party. I explained that this was normal operating procedure and we were going to have to adapt to your rather unpredictable schedule.''

Amanda grinned. She could just imagine the boy's indignation. Even though the streetwise runaway had adopted them about the same time they had gotten married, neither Amanda nor Joe knew much about his background. Pete refused to talk about where he was from or why he'd been living on the streets of Atlanta. He did, however, talk about almost everything else with an uncensored, colorful vocabulary that hadn't been taught by the Atlanta public schools.

From what they had gathered, the boy had never had a decent family of his own. Therefore he had certain idealistic fantasies about the way families were supposed to act. He was having difficulty getting Donelli and Amanda to fit his preconceived notions. Even before turning thirteen two weeks back, he had had no trouble expressing his views.

"How did he feel about your explanation for my tardiness?" Amanda asked.

"He muttered something entirely too cynical about women. Unfortunately, I had no readily accessible example to demonstrate to him that not all women march to their own drummer.''

Amanda caught an unmistakable edge in his voice—or

thought she did. "Is this really about Pete? Or is it about you?"

"Pete, definitely," he said without hesitation. "I've had longer to accept you the way you are."

Accept her, yes. That didn't stop him from worrying about her. "And I love you for that," she told him. Positive reinforcement, she congratulated herself. Wasn't that what all the pop psychology books touted as the way to modify behavior in either spouse or child?

"I love you, too."

"I'll be home soon."

"Whenever," he said agreeably. "Oh, and Amanda?"

"Yes?"

"Next time, call *before* you vanish on an assignment."

It sounded suspiciously like an order. Amanda automatically bristled until she reminded herself that not five seconds earlier she'd acknowledged Donelli's worrywort nature. It wouldn't kill her to relieve his mind with a phone call.

"Promise," she said finally, and hung up.

She vowed to hurry along the interview with Lou-Ellen. Fortunately the young woman was working in the mall's only music store, restocking the CDs. In an attempt to fit in, she was dressed in an outfit entirely inappropriate for someone who had to be the same age as Mary Allison's own thirty. Her skirt was too short, her top too tight, and her earrings entirely too flashy. Amanda was amazed that she and the elegant, classically tasteful Mary Allison had maintained contact.

She introduced herself to the woman. "Can you take a break for a minute?"

Lou-Ellen snapped her gum and nodded. "Sure. Just let me tell John I'll be out of the store."

John looked too bored to care where anyone was. Lou-Ellen's words barely seemed to register. She followed Amanda into the mall.

"Mind if we go to the food court?" she asked. "I could use a cup of coffee. It's been a long day."

"I'm sure it has been. I could use some coffee myself."

They picked up large coffees and a handful of chocolate-chip cookies and took them to a table. Amanda figured she was going to overdose on sugar if she kept talking to people in this crowd.

"Mrs. Watkins sent you to talk to me? How come?" Lou-Ellen asked, breaking off a chunk of cookie and popping it into her mouth. She eased off her shoes under the table and propped her feet on an extra chair.

"She thinks there's something strange about Mary Allison committing suicide. How do you feel about it?"

Lou-Ellen didn't look the least bit surprised by the question. "I gotta tell you, I was shocked," she said. "I mean Mary Allison is . . ." She stumbled on the tense, then looked as if she were about to cry. She swallowed hard and continued, "She *was* one of those people I've always admired. She had it together. She knew what she wanted by the time we were freshmen in high school, and she went after it."

"You mean the job in Washington?"

"The job, the man, the power. All of it."

"Why would she throw it all away, then?"

She looked genuinely baffled. "Beats me."

"Did you all talk much? Was she worried about anything? Depressed?"

Lou-Ellen laughed. "Mary Allison depressed? That's a good one. She could cheer up a room just by walking into it. No matter how bad things got when we were kids—and there were lots of times when money was tight or her mom was on her case—she never lost her smile. Sometimes it used to make me sick the way she could always see the good side of things. The rest of us were always griping about our parents, our teachers, whatever. Mary Allison never bitched about a thing."

"And that hadn't changed recently?"

Lou-Ellen looked thoughtful. "She might have been a little quieter than usual this last time, but it wasn't like she'd done a complete turnaround or something."

"You saw her this weekend before she died?"

"Friday night. We had dinner and looked at bridesmaid dresses. We giggled like a couple of fools over all that lace and chiffon. Felt like senior prom all over again, when she went with Billy Ray Lowry and I went with Buddy Tapponier. Those boys both have beer guts and no hair now, but we thought they were prime meat back then."

Before Lou-Ellen could take off down memory lane, Amanda quickly asked, "And she didn't mention being upset, maybe worried about her upcoming marriage or her job or something?"

"If she was, she didn't say a word to me. But I could read that girl like a book. I'd have known if something was wrong."

"Had you met Zack Downs?"

"Not until today at the funeral. It wasn't like they came down together on weekends to visit or anything. Mary Allison came home alone or her Mom went up to D.C."

Amanda sighed. "I guess that's it, then. If you think of anything, give me a call." She handed her one of her cards. "You going back now?"

"Nah. I've got another five minutes before I have to put these shoes back on. I'm not budging from here. Thanks for the coffee and cookies."

Amanda was almost out of the food court when Lou-Ellen caught up with her.

"There is one thing," she said, wiping at the coffee that had splashed onto her blouse as she'd run. She was barefoot, her shoes clutched in her other hand. "It happened a while back, so I'd almost forgotten about it. I went over to the house one Saturday when she was here in town, about a month ago, I guess. She got off the phone looking really upset. She mumbled something under her breath. I don't think she realized I was in the room. When I asked her what she'd meant, she looked real funny and told me she was just having a bad day."

"What did you overhear her say?"

"I think it was 'You're going to try that one time too many.' It sounded kinda like a threat."

"Any idea who she was talking to?"

"I can't absolutely swear to it, because she never said a name, but I got the feeling that she was talking to Senator Rawlings." She regarded Amanda hopefully. "Does that help at all?"

Amanda nodded. "It could help a lot."

As she drove home, she tried to imagine why one of the senator's most trusted aides would feel the need to threaten him.

C H A P T E R

Three

AMANDA was not used to having one man waiting up for her, much less two. She found Donelli and Pete in the kitchen, faced off across a checkerboard. They abandoned it when she walked through the door, but only Pete looked as if her late arrival were a personal affront. She aimed a daunting glare at the precocious thirteen-year-old.

"No lectures, okay? It's been a long day."

"But . . ." he protested.

"Don't waste your breath," Donelli advised him. His gaze searched Amanda's face. "What did you find out?"

"Mrs. Watkins and Lou-Ellen Kinsale, one of Mary Allison's bridal attendants, both agree that there wasn't a sign last weekend that Mary Allison was depressed, much less suicidal. In fact, she was shopping for dresses for the wedding."

Pete's dour expression perked up immediately. "You working a murder case?"

Amanda exchanged a look with Donelli. Her response came slowly. "I'm beginning to think that's a very real possibility."

"Any evidence?" asked Joe, whose well-trained skepticism required facts, not gut instinct or speculation.

"Intuition, so far," she admitted. "Her mother's convinced of it, though. And Lou-Ellen overheard Mary Allison say something that might have been construed as a threat against the senator."

"How serious a threat? Did she actually threaten to kill him or expose him?"

"No, it was more along the lines that he was pushing her too far on something."

"Whom did she allegedly make this comment to?"

"Lou-Ellen thinks the senator himself."

"She *thinks* that or she knows it?"

Amanda shot him an irritated look. "Okay, it could have been someone on his staff," she agreed reluctantly, not liking the way he was neatly disposing of her best evidence. "What's for dinner?"

"Pasta, and don't change the subject just because you're losing," he said. "Amanda, surely you don't think that Senator Rawlings or even anyone on his staff had something to do with that woman's death?"

"Why do you say it like that?" she asked with an undeniably defensive note in her voice. She didn't want to admit that it didn't make a lot of sense.

Searching the refrigerator, she found the cold pasta in an airtight container. She grabbed a fork from the drawer and, still standing, proceeded to eat the pasta just as it was.

An Italian to the core and a man for whom pasta was a national treasure, Joe flinched, stood up, and took the container away, jamming it into the microwave. Even that offended him, but apparently he could tell she was in no mood to wait while he made up a fresh batch. He put the now steaming pasta into a bowl, tossed it gently, then placed it on the table.

"Sit. Eat," he instructed, and went back to the seat opposite her. "Now, let's get back to the senator. I say that your theory sucks because we're talking about a highly regarded member of Congress, not some third-rate hood."

"Making it to Capitol Hill is hardly proof of high moral character."

"The way the media bird-dogs these guys these days, I'd say most of their sins are exposed."

"Sooner or later," she agreed. "In his case, maybe it's later. After all, he was involved in that scheme to get illegal arms shipments into Iraq. I found that out firsthand, when I investigated the shady dealings of that foreign bank here in Atlanta. All the trails led straight to him. Remember?"

"He was involved at the behest of the government," Joe reminded her. "It was a CIA operation. He wasn't involved for personal gain."

"Even so, it was evidence that he's capable of being sneaky and underhanded when it suits his purposes. Who knows how he might retaliate if someone was about to expose his shenanigans."

"What shenanigans?" Joe inquired patiently.

Amanda sighed, conceding Donelli's victory . . . for the moment. "I don't know that yet," she admitted.

Pete was listening intently. "Are you talking about that old guy who's on TV all the time?"

"By your standards, there are a lot of old guys on TV," Amanda reminded him. "To hear you tell it, some of them are Joe's and my age."

Pete wasn't distracted by the accusation. "You know which one I mean," he retorted. "Senator Rawlings, right? I've seen him around."

Amanda regarded him doubtfully. "And just where have you bumped into the senator?"

"Sometimes he eats in that coffee shop downtown near Peachtree Center," Pete replied, sounding every bit as smug as Donelli when his patience won out over her impetuous behavior to unearth a critical clue. "I used to go there when I picked up a couple of bucks. He always has some babe with him. I saw him there lots with that woman who smashed into that tree, the one you're talking about."

Amanda tended to forget that Pete was not a typical teenager, absorbed with video games and girls. Determined never to return home and flatly refusing even to tell them where home was, he'd been living by his wits and whatever odd jobs he managed to pick up. He was savvy and observant. She sorted through the stack of old newspapers waiting to be taken out until she found the one with the picture of Mary Allison Watkins.

"This woman?"

"Yeah, sure. And some blonde, too. A real class act. She reminded me of that woman who used to be in the movies, the one who died after she married some prince."

"Grace Kelly," Joe supplied, regarding Pete in amazement.

"Yeah. Now, *she* was some dame," Pete said with feeling. He reached for Amanda's half-empty bowl of pasta. "You done?"

"It's all yours," she said. She decided that Pete had seen entirely too many old Humphrey Bogart and James Cagney films if he was referring to women as "dames." He also had a gleam of approval in his eyes that was entirely too masculine and too grown-up. She wondered worriedly if it was too late for him to become a normal teenage boy, who played softball or basketball after school and went to the mall with friends on the weekends just to pick up girls. She looked into those world-weary eyes and decided with regret that it probably was.

He watched her expectantly. "So what are we going to do next?"

"*We* aren't going to do anything," she said firmly.

"You're going to stay right here and help Joe, just the way you've been doing."

"Come on, he doesn't need me. He's got all these other guys to help him. You're the one who gets in trouble if someone's not looking after you."

Fortunately Donelli didn't comment on the truth of that observation. Instead he told Pete, "I need you handling the sales at the produce stand out on the highway. There's no one else I can trust with that."

Pete's chest puffed up with pride at the mention of trust, though he still looked as if he'd rather be chasing a murderer with Amanda. "We'll still put our heads together, right?" he asked. "I mean, I know all about bad guys. You need somebody like me who understands the criminal mind."

From anyone else with such an angelic face and painfully thin body just beginning an adolescent spurt of growth, the remark might have been laughable. Coming from Pete, it was probably dead-on truth. Amanda fought the desire to ruffle his hair or pull him into a hug. Either gesture would have embarrassed him.

"You will be my chief consultant," she promised.

Pete beamed with satisfaction. Donelli regarded them both with that worried expression he got when he knew Amanda was headed for trouble.

"What's next?" he asked.

"If I can get Oscar's okay, I'm going to Washington."

He nodded, looking resigned. "I was afraid of that.

Have you checked to make sure that Rawlings and his staff aren't here in town?''

''Not yet, but Mrs. Watkins said Zack Downs and one of the senator's aides were headed back right after they left her house tonight. I assume Rawlings has gone back, too. I'll call his office first thing in the morning to double-check before I book a flight.''

''Hey, wait a minute,'' Pete protested. ''What good am I going to do you if I'm here and you're in Washington? That's a long way away, right?''

''Not so far,'' Amanda said, just as Donelli said, ''Far enough.'' Glancing at Pete, he added, ''I'll show you on the map.''

Pete was already shaking his head. ''I don't like this, you guys. She's going to be up there all alone with a murderer.''

Donelli held back a rueful grin. ''See what you've done? The boy already has your suspicious nature, and he's only lived with us a couple of months.''

Amanda dismissed the accusation. ''He could probably give me lessons in suspicion.'' She did, however, dutifully remind Pete that they weren't certain a murder had been committed.

''So you'll be out with some dude, asking all these nosy questions, and then you'll find out? Sounds like a good way to get killed, if you ask me,'' he scoffed. He appealed to Joe. ''You can't let her do this, man.''

Joe grinned. ''You try to stop her, then. I know better.''

Pete was not amused. ''Aw, man, this sucks,'' he announced. He walked out, letting the screen door slam behind him.

Amanda winced. "Why do I have this awful feeling that the next time I see him will be on the steps of the Capitol?"

CHAPTER

Four

AUGUST in Washington felt like the steamroom of the worst gym Amanda had ever been in. There was no relief from the oppressive heat and humidity, not even a faint stirring of a breeze or a thundercloud on the horizon. The air actually had a visible texture to it, shimmering above the blazing sidewalks.

As she stood outside waiting for the Metro to take her from National Airport into Washington, perspiration soaked right through her blouse. She regretted the decision to rush up here to ask questions no one was going to want to answer. She could have just stayed in Atlanta and waited for the senator and his staff to return over Labor Day weekend, as Gregory Fine had told her they would. Of course, the last time she'd confronted the senator in his rose garden about those illegal arms heading to Iraq, he'd called the FBI on her.

More important, waiting would have cost her the hard-won cover story position Oscar had reluctantly agreed this morning to hold for her. Waiting around for her prospective sources to come to her might even have cost her a chance to pursue the story at all. It would have suggested to Oscar that she wasn't fully committed to the investigation after all. As it was, he thought she was courting a libel suit. It wasn't his favorite form of journalistic sport.

"If Senator Rawlings gets a whiff of this stink you intend to raise, he'll haul you up on charges so fast it'll make your head swim," Oscar had warned right before he'd reluctantly okayed the trip to Washington. "You go slow. Don't make any insinuations. Keep your questions as offhand as you can."

"The senator is not the first public figure I've ever attempted to nail," she had reminded him. "I know what I'm doing."

Oscar had nodded. "You're known for your subtlety all right. I seem to recall that the corrupt judge you went after in New York tried to kill you in return for all the unwanted publicity you heaped on him."

"Well, yes," she conceded, shuddering at the memory. "But I had him dead to rights, and he had nothing left to lose. Rawlings won't do that."

"Oh? You think he's too much of a southern gentleman? If that's it, I must be confused about your angle here. I thought you were suggesting he had something to do with that poor woman's death, a woman he knew and trusted." He regarded her intently. "Whereas you are a woman who has driven that man crazy from the first second you met him.''

Amanda winced. ''I see your point. I'll make my inquiries discreet.''

Discretion was not exactly her strong suit, especially when dealing with powerful figures. After she had dropped off her bags at the Hay-Adams Hotel on Lafayette Square, Amanda decided that she'd better try to arrange a meeting with Mary Allison's maid of honor, Valerie LaPalma, first. She'd tell her it was background for a profile of Mary Allison. That ought to be innocuous and unthreatening enough.

Amanda went straight over to Capitol Hill, located the senator's office, and strolled in as if her arrival were no more than a drop-in visit from a Georgia constituent. Gregory Fine, who considered most reporters to be pushy, arrogant, and sworn natural enemies of all decent public servants, glanced up from his desk in the office to the left of the senator's, took one startled look at her, and bustled through the connecting door into the senator's inner sanctum. No doubt he'd rushed off to report that the worst of the media vultures had just landed. His quick retreat left a harried receptionist to handle whatever Amanda had on her mind. The coward.

Actually, though, Fine's departure suited Amanda's purposes quite nicely. The middle-aged woman who looked up at her wore a simple gray suit, a silk blouse, silver jewelry, and a friendly expression that indicated she had absolutely no idea who Amanda was, much less Amanda's persona non grata status with her bosses, neither of whom had taken kindly to Amanda's interference in their tidy little CIA arms scheme.

Amanda wished she could keep it that way. But even if she didn't reveal her name or her profession, Greg Fine was bound to spread the word before she could do too much unobtrusive snooping. She guessed she had maybe ten, fifteen minutes at best, and that was only if she could overcome her own personal ethics, which required her always to identify herself to a prospective source. She figured entrapment was no more savory for a journalist than it was for a cop.

"May I help you?" the receptionist inquired pleasantly. "Did you have an appointment with the senator?"

"No, actually I was looking for one of his aides, Valerie LaPalma. Is she available?"

The woman's smile faltered. "No, I'm afraid she's taken a few leave days."

"Because of her friend's death, I suppose?"

"Oh, did you know Mary Allison?"

Amanda shook her head. "I'm afraid not."

With her conscience already screaming at her, she removed a business card from her purse and handed it to the receptionist. "I am working on a profile about her, though. I've spoken with her mother and a close friend in Atlanta, but I really need to learn more about her life here in Washington."

The woman suddenly looked downright uneasy. "I really don't know what anyone here could tell you. Mary Allison kept to herself."

"But she'd worked for the senator for nearly ten years. Surely you or Mr. Fine or the senator knew her well."

"I didn't work all that closely with her myself," the woman said, her voice definitely chilly now and her expression losing the last pretense of friendliness. "I'm afraid I would have nothing to say."

"Perhaps you could put me in touch with Ms. LaPalma, then," Amanda suggested.

"It would be against policy for me to give you a home number," the receptionist reported dutifully.

Amanda glanced down at the nameplate on her desk. "No problem, Ms. Wilcox. I have a home number. I thought perhaps you would know where she might have gone if she's on leave."

"I have no idea where to locate her. For all I know she could be at home."

The runaround was beginning to test Amanda's always fragile patience. "What if you needed to get in touch with her in an emergency?"

"I wouldn't be the one to do that. If you'd like to speak with Mr. Fine, I could buzz him."

Amanda really didn't want to start her interviews with the officious chief of staff, but she couldn't see any way around it, especially since he already knew she was in the office. At least he didn't know why she was there. That morning she'd merely asked him what the senator's travel itinerary was over the next couple of weeks, hinting that she'd hoped to catch up with him next time he was in Atlanta. There might have been the slightest innuendo that she was considering a major profile of the state's senior politician in anticipation of November's election. Fine had supplied his schedule in a tone that had moved from suspicious to fawning so quickly, Amanda was amazed his tongue hadn't wound up with verbal whiplash.

Apparently, though, her sudden arrival in Washington on the heels of that inquiry had given him second thoughts, even if he still had no idea what she was really after. She figured it was too late to catch him completely off guard, but catching him before the receptionist could spill the beans was the only hope she had.

"If he has a minute, that would be great," she said, practically choking on her own feigned enthusiasm. She stood close by so she could hear precisely what Ms. Wilcox said to him. Fortunately the woman kept it brief and to the point, saying only that a reporter wished to speak to him.

The chief of staff emerged not five seconds later. Just in case Amanda was here to do a glorious puff piece on the candidate, he had a smile plastered across his narrow little face. She made a bet with herself that she could wipe it off with one question.

"Ms. Roberts," he said politely. "I had no idea when we spoke this morning that we'd be seeing you so soon. What can we do for you?"

"I'd like to chat with you and the senator about Mary Allison Watkins," she said.

Sure enough, his expression soured. "Why would you want to do that?"

"It's a powerful story. A young woman on the verge of attaining all of her dreams suddenly commits suicide. Surely you can see why people would want to understand what went wrong."

"Mary Allison obviously had a character flaw of some kind that none of us had detected."

Amanda didn't have to feign her incredulity at the statement. But she measured her words. "An astute man such as yourself surely wouldn't miss something that serious."

He looked as if he weren't quite sure how to take the comment. Apparently he decided it was meant as a compliment. He preened. "I do pride myself on being able to judge people. That's why I'm of value to the senator, but I mistakenly assumed that what we saw of Mary Allison around here was all there was to her. Apparently there was another side she kept hidden."

"And what side was that?"

"The despondency, of course. Perhaps if she had gotten treatment," he suggested with a hint of sorrow. He even bowed his head slightly, a man praying for forgiveness, no doubt.

Amanda decided not to pursue what was clearly the official line on Mary Allison's death. Instead she asked, "She was doing her job up until the end, though? She wasn't letting things slide?"

He looked positively horrified by the suggestion. "Absolutely not. I wouldn't have tolerated that, and neither would the senator,'' he said.

Based on his indignant expression, he was clearly unaware that he'd just made a case against his own explanation for some hidden depression. If Mary Allison had been as bad off as he'd suggested, surely her work would have suffered. There probably would have been unexplained absences, slipshod reports, something to indicate that things were not normal.

Instead he'd painted a picture of a responsible woman who was coping with her daily life just as she always had. Amanda wondered if the senator would be any more forthcoming. She figured she might as well try while she was already in his office and before Gregory Fine had time to prep him thoroughly for her questions. God forbid they had time to put a slick PR spin on the answers. She'd never get at the truth.

''I certainly appreciate your take on the situation, but I wonder if I might speak with the senator for just a moment. I realize I don't have an appointment,'' she said, managing to sound meek and solicitous. She figured that would work better on this occasion than the kind of confrontative demands she'd shouted the last time she'd barged past Gregory Fine and into the senator's inner sanctum. Oscar would have been proud, if he'd heard her. Donelli would have been astonished.

Fine looked as if he'd rather ship her off to a D.C. jail, but he nodded curtly. ''I'll see what I can do.'' A moment later he motioned her into Senator Blaine Rawlings's office.

Dressed in a handsomely tailored navy blue suit, a pale blue shirt, and red, white, and blue–striped tie, the sixty-eight-year-old white-haired senior senator from Georgia was in his element behind a huge mahogany desk flanked on either side by a United States flag and one from his own home state. He looked as if he'd been dressed up for a photo opportunity. Back home he tended toward khaki pants, flashy suspenders, and gardening gloves.

He beamed at Amanda as if they'd parted on positively friendly terms the last time they'd met. Perhaps he considered that they had, since he'd gotten his way. *Inside Atlanta* had held off on printing Amanda's exposé of the government's involvement in an attempt to overthrow the Iraqi leadership until the last scenes had been played out in Baghdad.

"My dear, you're looking lovely," he drawled.

Amanda knew all too well that that lazy charm could be replaced in an instant by icy disdain. Under all that *"aw shucks"* demeanor lurked a quick intelligence and cutthroat political astuteness. He'd been chairman of the powerful Senate Foreign Relations Committee for years, a position that rewarded clout and savvy.

"I'm sorry to barge in on you, Senator."

"Nonsense. I'm always happy to speak with a member of the media."

He shot a glance toward his aide, probably to see if he

was laying it on too thick. He should have looked more closely at Amanda. She was trying not to gag.

"So, what brings you all the way to Washington?"

"Mary Allison Watkins," she said bluntly.

If her announcement threw him, it didn't show. He nodded sagely. "A tragic situation. Absolutely tragic. She was a great addition to my staff. She will be sorely missed, I can tell you that. That funeral yesterday like to broke my heart."

Amanda figured he was ready to go on and on about the good always dying young. She cut him off. "Why did you hire her?"

He regarded her in confusion. "Why would you ask that? She was qualified, of course. And I like to hire people from the home state whenever possible. Actually, I don't do the hiring myself. Greg here sees to most of that. He knows the kind of people we need around here."

Amanda glanced at the aide. "What did you see in Mary Allison that convinced you she could do the job? As I understand it, when she came here she had very little experience, just a college degree."

"She was a quick study," he said at once. "That's always what I look for. And she was ambitious. People who are smart and want to get ahead make the best employees."

"Because they'll do whatever it takes," Amanda wondered aloud before she could censor herself.

"Because they are aggressive, yes," Fine said, putting

a better face on the same thing. "And they are willing to work long hours. Working for a senator is not a nine-to-five job. Anyone who thinks that won't last long."

"What exactly did Mary Allison do?"

The senator fielded that one, probably because he considered the question so innocuous. "She worked on policy research, made recommendations to Greg and me about positions that would be in the best interests of the people of Georgia. She helped design several bills we introduced over the years."

"That sounds like a lot of power."

"It was," Rawlings agreed. "I trusted Mary Allison implicitly. She made her assessments based on fact, not emotion. That's a hard thing for a woman . . . for anyone to do."

Amanda wondered at the slip of the tongue. It didn't particularly surprise her to learn that Blaine Rawlings had a chauvinistic streak. Many southern men of his generation did. It did startle her that he was apparently aware it was not politically correct.

"You were fond of her, then?"

He seemed uneasy with her phrasing. Gregory Fine looked positively horrified, though he was trying valiantly to cover his reaction. Again, Amanda wondered why.

"I am *fond*, as you put it, of all my staff," Rawlings said curtly. "We're family around here. That's why we're all devastated about Mary Allison's death."

Amanda hadn't noticed that Ms. Wilcox was particularly devastated, but she let it pass. "I understand that one of your assistants, Valerie LaPalma, has taken some time off.''

Rawlings glanced at his aide. ''I wasn't aware of that.''

''She and Mary Allison were good friends,'' Fine explained to both of them. ''Naturally she has taken this even harder than the rest of us. We felt it would be best if she had a few days alone to cope with her grief.''

Something in the explanation struck Amanda as odd. ''Did she ask for the time off, or did you suggest it?''

''I believe I offered her compassionate leave time, the sort we grant for the deaths of family members,'' Fine said as if he'd had to think back weeks, rather than twenty-four hours ago, maybe even less. ''She agreed that she needed a few extra days to collect herself.''

''Did she go out of town?''

His gaze narrowed suspiciously. ''Why all the questions about Ms. LaPalma?''

''Obviously because she knew Mary Allison well,'' Amanda replied, meeting his gaze evenly. ''Talking with her will be critical for any story I do. Naturally I'm wondering how and when I can get in touch with her.''

''I believe she'll be back week after next.''

''Did she leave town?'' she asked again.

''We didn't discuss her plans, and if we had, I don't believe it would be appropriate to share them with you,'' he snapped impatiently.

The senator held up his hand in a warning gesture, even as he smiled apologetically at Amanda. ''I'm sure you understand that we are under a great deal of stress. Anytime there's a suicide those left behind wonder what they could have done to prevent it. It's a terrible burden.''

''I'm sure you've given it a great deal of thought yourself, Senator. Could you have done something differently in Mary Allison's case?'' she asked.

He lifted his gaze to meet hers. His eyes were bleak. ''I wish I knew that, young lady. I surely do wish I knew that.''

Watching his expression closely, Amanda thought that might have been the first totally sincere remark she'd ever heard Blaine Rawlings make.

C H A P T E R

Five

AMANDA left the senator's office feeling more depressed and confused than she had before she'd made the trip. At first glance, Blaine Rawlings and his chief of staff were appropriately shaken by Mary Allison's death. They seemed to be mourning her. The operative phrase, though, was *"seemed to be."*

Right at the end, when she had looked into the senator's eyes, she had seen honest grief over the loss of someone dear to him, someone he'd perhaps thought of almost as a daughter.

It was his tone she had found troubling. She had detected a faint hint of defensiveness that shouldn't have been there. She hadn't asked any truly tough questions. She hadn't so much as hinted that she found anything suspicious in the death.

So, she wondered, why had everyone from the receptionist to Gregory Fine to the senator himself answered so guardedly? It was more than the natural response to a reporter's inquiries. They were all hiding something. She was sure of it. But what? Were they collectively keeping some dark but relatively innocent little secret, or could they all be conspiring to cover up a murder?

Amanda guessed that Valerie LaPalma was her best bet for finding out. She called her apartment, got an answering machine with a simple message that said nothing to indicate if she was in town or away, and left a message asking Valerie to call her as soon as possible at the Hay-Adams.

Not five minutes later, when she was about to order dinner from room service and spend the evening delving more deeply into the backgrounds of her sources, her phone rang.

"So, *ma chérie,* you come to town and do not call an old friend," Armand LeConte accused gently.

For a remark delivered so nonchalantly, Amanda thought it took on an amazingly sexual tone thanks to his delightful French accent. She debated how she felt about hearing from him.

"How on earth did you know where I was?" she asked the arms merchant who'd helped her on that illegal arms story several months back and who had pursued her with wicked French charm until the very day she'd married Donelli. She suspected, given his Gallic views on marriage and the acceptability of discreet affairs, that he wouldn't give up even now.

"Surely you know by now that I have my ways to

accomplish anything," he replied. "Have you made plans for dinner?"

"I was about to order room service and go over my interview notes. I also have to go through the background faxes my research assistant sent," she said, referring to the material Jenny Lee had hastily assembled not only on Rawlings, but on Greg Fine as well.

"And waste an opportunity to spend an evening with an admirer? I cannot allow it, *ma chérie*. I will pick you up in one hour. Wear something positively ravishing."

The offer of dinner was at least marginally less tempting than the opportunity to pick his brain. "My travel wardrobe doesn't run to ravishing," she retorted. "I suppose I can find something that won't embarrass you, though."

"Bon," he announced. "Good. You are not arguing. One hour, *ma chérie*. I will look forward to it."

The minute she'd hung up, guilt had Amanda dialing home. There would be no secrets from Donelli, not ever, though confessing to an innocent dinner made her wonder if she weren't making too much of the old attraction she had briefly felt for LeConte. Surely her wedding vows had wiped all lascivious thoughts of other men from her head. Besides, if necessary, she could make a very powerful case that this was a purely business dinner. Armand had an amazing array of political connections given his somewhat shady profession.

"How'd your first day go?" Donelli inquired.

"If I learned anything, I'm not bright enough to figure it out yet."

"You having dinner with LeConte?"

Amanda almost dropped the phone. "How'd you know about that?"

"I called him. Since I couldn't be there, I figured you ought to have somebody to rely on in a pinch. Knowing how much you hated that bodyguard he sent trailing after you once before, I knew you'd never call him yourself."

That was one reason, Amanda admitted to herself. There was another.

"Then there's your sometimes overly active sense of loyalty to me," he said.

That was the other one. "Oh," she replied meekly.

"I trust you, Amanda."

Well, she thought, wasn't that nice? Actually, it was just a little insulting. Wouldn't a smidgen of jealousy have been more satisfying?

Why? she asked herself. So she could rant and rave about it? She dismissed her reaction with disgust.

"Thank you," she said finally.

Donelli chuckled. "You can even enjoy yourself, if you want to."

"I don't need your permission," she grumbled.

"Oh, really?" he said with evident amusement. "Gotta run. The spaghetti water is boiling over."

"Wait a minute," she shouted.

"Good grief, Amanda, you don't need to blast my eardrum out."

"Sorry. I thought you were hanging up. Where's Pete?"

Donelli laughed, obviously guessing why she was sounding so worried. "Asleep on the sofa. I had him weeding all day today. It wore him out. Kept his mind off being left behind, too. Just don't stay away too long or I can't promise to be accountable for his whereabouts. We have plenty of proof that the kid is resourceful enough to make his way to D.C., if he gets it into his head you need him."

"I'll be home as soon as I can," she promised.

After they'd hung up, Amanda stared at the phone and wondered how she'd ever gotten so lucky. She'd never expected to find a man who understood not only the importance of her career, but her impetuous nature as well *and* trusted her. In fact, it had been Joe's gut-deep certainty that they could make marriage work that had overcome her wariness. So far, at least, he'd been proven right.

"I understand you've been assigned to guard duty," she told Armand when she was settled into the luxurious leather interior of his limousine.

He gave her an enigmatic smile. "It is, what is the expression, like asking the wolf to protect the henhouse, yes?"

She grinned. "Something like that."

He scanned her with those penetrating, crystal blue eyes that could reduce an enemy to nothing and a woman to whimpers. "You are well, *ma chérie?* You look lovely. Marriage must agree with you."

"So far, so good."

"And the boy? You are enjoying the unexpected role of mother?"

Amanda thought about that. She wasn't sure exactly how she felt about Pete. She didn't think it was precisely maternal. But then, what did she know about motherhood? She did know that she cared what happened to the teenager. She was fascinated by the twists and turns of his lively mind. And in that one instant in her kitchen a few months back when Pete's life had been threatened, she had finally known what it would take to make her pull the trigger on the gun she'd always hated owning.

"I don't think I would have wanted to miss the experience of having him in our lives," she told Armand. "He is a unique young man."

"So I understand," he replied dryly. "Now, what is this important story that brings you to Washington?"

"Joe didn't tell you?"

"Only that it might prove dangerous."

"That's good to know. I'd hate to think my husband was giving away all of my professional secrets."

"He was very circumspect. However, if I am to help, I should know more, yes?"

Amanda wondered about that. Armand had extensive sources all over the world, many of them powerful men on Capitol Hill. He counted Blaine Rawlings among his friends. How much would he be inclined to reveal about his friend?

"Did you ever meet Valérie LaPalma?" she asked, deciding that his question called for a little circumspection of her own. Judging from the predatory gleam that immediately sparked in his eyes, Amanda guessed that he knew the elegant Valerie very well. "How could I even ask? She is beautiful, right? And available. Of course you would know her."

His lips curved in a satisfied smile. "You are jealous, just a little?"

"I am married. Of course I am not jealous," she insisted testily. "Do you know her or not?"

"We are acquainted," he said.

"Define 'acquainted.' "

"You would not really expect me to elaborate, would you, *ma chérie? A* gentleman would not, *n'est-ce, pas?*"

Amanda groaned. "I knew it. Okay, where is she? I need to speak with her."

He hesitated, then shrugged. "Her comings and goings are no concern of mine. Is she not at work?"

Amanda studied his face for signs that he was evading a direct answer. He looked perfectly innocent. Of course, a man who traded in guns and claimed he was no more than a simple businessman had to have perfected the fine art of the innocent expression. That hesitation, however slight, though, had given him away. He, like everyone else, knew something he wasn't saying. Damn him.

"No, she is not at work," she said, regarding him intently. "She's on leave. No one at the office seems inclined to tell me how to track her down. I've left a message for her. Hopefully, she'll call before I have to go back to Atlanta.''

He sighed. "Perhaps I could make some inquiries. It is important that you speak with her?''

"Very important," Amanda assured him as they pulled up in front of the Jockey Club, one of Washington's favorite hangouts for over thirty years.

Armand exchanged a few quiet words with his driver before escorting her inside. "Perhaps we will know something by later this evening," he reassured her.

Over a dinner that materialized as if by magic, Armand entertained her with outrageous stories about his beloved daughter, who was growing more precocious by the day. "I have threatened to ship her away to a Swiss boarding school if she does not behave, but, alas, she does not seem to take me seriously," he said with an exaggerated sigh of resignation.

"You would no more send Noelle away than you would take up selling vacuum cleaners instead of weapons," Amanda accused. "You adore that child."

Some terribly nostalgic thought turned his expression solemn. It was the kind of haunting look that had entranced women the world over, including Amanda. She'd been wise enough, however, to escape its lure, if not its fascination. She'd always hoped that one day he would tell her the story of Noelle's mother, but he'd kept silent on that as he did on most things about himself. The hints of tragedy, like those of secret deals and dangerous undercurrents, were always there.

"She will have to go away one day, *ma chérie*. My solitary life is no good for a young girl. She needs a woman's influence."

Amanda touched his hand. "No more than she needs your love, Armand."

He glanced at her fingers resting on his, then closed his hand around hers and lifted it to his lips. "Ah, *ma chérie*, I think my heart broke on the day you wed. You have the intrepid spirit and romantic soul I would wish for my daughter."

Amanda's pulse hammered, as always when Armand chose to be gallant and charming, but she knew the sentiment was shallow, as transitory as a wisp of smoke. In the end he would share his heart with no woman, except perhaps his beloved daughter. She forced a teasing note into her voice. "You aren't looking for a wife, Armand. You want a nanny."

His eyes sparkled wickedly at the accusation. "*Ma chérie*, you do not know me nearly so well as you think you do."

An odd little tremor of excitement, dark and dangerous, pulsed through Amanda. Then she thought of Donelli's quiet strength and dependability and knew that she could never have exchanged it for the passionate uncertainty of a man like Armand, whose ethics were no better than they had to be. She wondered if Donelli had realized in setting up this dinner that she needed to make that discovery for herself. Probably. Her husband frequently demonstrated that he knew her better than she knew herself. In some respects that was a damned nuisance.

As they lingered over coffee, Armand gave an almost imperceptible nod toward the waiter. A phone appeared. He placed a call, mumbled something in French too rapid for Amanda to translate, then dialed again. When he'd spoken to whoever answered, he handed the receiver to Amanda.

"Dessert, *ma chérie*." At Amanda's puzzled expression, he added, "Ms. LaPalma."

"You are a wizard," she murmured as she took the phone. He sat back, watching her with tolerant amusement.

"Armand and Henri say I can trust you," Valerie La-Palma said.

As Donelli had reminded her earlier, Amanda knew all about Henri. To her chagrin, Armand had once assigned him to play bodyguard to her. He'd trailed her all over Atlanta, despite her best efforts to have him called off. She wondered how he fit into this particular scenario. Was Valerie LaPalma in some danger?

"Could we arrange to meet?" she asked.

There was a faint hesitation. "I'm not sure that would be wise."

"You said yourself that you've been told I'm trustworthy."

"Even so, I really prefer to keep my whereabouts unknown for the moment."

"Are you on leave because of Mary Allison's death, Ms. LaPalma? Or are you hiding out?"

The choked laugh that greeted the questions bore an unmistakable edge of hysteria. "I'm not sure it's possible anymore to tell the difference."

C H A P T E R

Six

AMANDA was caught in a very real quandary. She didn't want to compromise Valerie LaPalma's safety, if that was an issue, but she needed to talk to her in depth and in person. That was even more important now that she was virtually a hundred percent certain that Valerie knew something about Mary Allison's death and that what she knew had sent her into hiding.

"Please, let me have Armand bring me to you," she pleaded. "Obviously he knows where you are. He can even blindfold me so I won't know where we're going." She glanced across the dinner table and caught the amused glint in his eyes as he sipped his espresso.

"A trifle melodramatic, *ma chérie*," he commented.

"I'll do whatever it takes," she said curtly.

He observed her intently for a full minute, then nodded. "As you wish." He took the phone from her and spoke to

Valerie, his tone reassuring, though Amanda could pick out only a few words of the muffled exchange. He hung up within seconds. "Shall we go?"

"She agreed?"

He shrugged off her amazement. "It was not difficult. Only you have withstood the power of my persuasion, *ma cherie.*"

"That must have been a blow to your ego."

"One from which I may never recover," he agreed readily.

Despite the glib banter, Amanda couldn't help wondering what Armand had actually said to persuade the reluctant Valerie to see her. Did he hold some power over Valerie, aside from the obvious effect of his incredible charm and magnetism? As always, the dynamics of the relationship intrigued Amanda. She wondered if she would more fully understand it after meeting the senator's aide in person.

As they walked outside, Armand's limousine cruised to the curb. This time Henri was behind the wheel. He nodded to Amanda. "Ms. Roberts."

"Good evening, Henri."

Armand handed her into the limo. "Henri, you will take Ms. Roberts to see Ms. LaPalma. She is expecting her." He glanced at Amanda. "There will be no need to blindfold her. I'm sure we can trust her discretion."

"You're not coming?" Amanda asked, surprised and oddly disappointed. She also had a feeling the persuasive and trusted Armand might have wheedled answers from

Valerie LePalma that she would keep from a prying journalist.

"You will be quite safe and comfortable with Henri," he assured her. "I have matters here in Washington to which I must attend."

It wasn't until they had pulled away from the curb, the big car almost silent in the night, that Amanda caught the full meaning of Armand's comment. She rolled down the window between herself and her escort, a term she much preferred to the one that more precisely described Henri's actual duties.

"Henri, just where are we going?"

"To the airport, Ms. Roberts."

"The airport?" she repeated incredulously. "Why?"

"Ms. LaPalma is vacationing at Monsieur LeConte's château in France. His jet will take us. We should be there by morning."

Amanda debated leaping from the limo in the middle of the Key Bridge, then sank back against the luxurious leather. Did it really matter that she was about to fly halfway around the world to conduct an interview? Nothing had changed. She still needed Valerie LaPalma's insights into Mary Allison's death if she was to pursue this story. Now it also seemed she needed to know why Valerie herself had felt the need to hide out on the other side of the Atlantic under the protection of an international arms dealer.

"You are okay, Ms. Roberts?"

She sighed. "Just peachy, Henri. Just peachy."

* * *

It wasn't until she was halfway across the Atlantic that it occurred to Amanda that French authorities were not going to admit her to their country without her passport, which was tucked into some box that had yet to be unpacked back in Georgia. Given the last time she'd actually had to use it, it was probably outdated as well. She glanced at the hawk-nosed man across the aisle of the luxurious small plane. Apparently used to the whims of his unpredictable boss, he appeared as relaxed as if this were a trip he'd been planning for weeks.

"Henri?"

Without turning his head toward her, he replied, "Yes, Ms. Roberts."

"I seem to be caught without my passport."

"That will not be a problem, madame. Monsieur LeConte anticipated the situation and made the necessary arrangements."

Of course he had, Amanda thought. Armand was the kind of man who thought of everything, who never let a technicality stand in the way of his wishes. It was probably best not to think of how many people had been bribed or otherwise persuaded in order to make this spur-of-the-moment trip happen. Oscar would probably have heart failure when he found out. He'd be torn between the ethical necessity of repaying every penny and the impact on his travel budget for the next half dozen years.

On that thought, she allowed herself to drift to sleep. She was awakened hours later by the scent of freshly brewed coffee and warm croissants. Henri deposited a tray in front of her. Apparently there was no end to the man's skills. She knew for a fact how efficiently and unemotionally he could dispose of an inconvenient enemy.

"We will be landing in about forty-five minutes, just about eight o'clock in the morning in Paris. A driver will meet us and take us to Ms. LaPalma."

He said it as if it could be accomplished with a snap of the fingers, and to Amanda's amazement, it was. They were whisked through customs, packed into yet another luxurious car, and cruising through the French countryside in a matter of minutes. No one batted an eye at her lack of papers, accepting her Georgia driver's license and her press pass as identification, then welcoming her with Gallic curtness.

The château, like Armand's estate in Virginia, was set in scenic surroundings so lovely that they took Amanda's breath away. A quaint village with impossibly narrow, twisting streets and whitewashed houses with red-tiled roofs nestled at the base of a hillside. Beyond that, fields were abloom with flowers. They curved up a narrow, winding road, then turned into a gate virtually hidden amid a stand of ancient trees. She could feel the pull on the car's engine as they climbed higher and higher before emerging on grounds that swept away from the grey château like a blanket of green velvet that had been spread out for an elegant picnic.

The house was not at all what Amanda had expected. It was old and charming, not the intimidating, massive structure she had envisioned. Flowers bloomed every-where, a heady abundance of every kind imaginable, and the windows of the house were open to catch their fragrance.

"I believe we will find Ms. LaPalma in the back," Henri said, leading her along a well-worn dirt path beside the house.

Amanda wondered how he could possibly know that, then remembered the series of hushed calls he'd made on the car phone, while she'd been absorbed in her first impressions of France. Obviously everyone from Ms. Le-Palma to Armand knew they'd arrived safely. Donelli probably even knew. Armand would have felt duty-bound to keep him informed of her whereabouts. Hell, they'd probably conspired to whisk her off to someplace where they figured she, too, would be out of danger, she thought, suddenly annoyed.

Her mood lasted no longer than it took to turn the corner of the house and see Valerie LaPalma sitting at a glass-topped wrought-iron table, which had been set for two. Dressed in jeans and a white T-shirt, her hair pulled back in a ponytail, she was sipping a glass of orange juice as she awaited Amanda's arrival.

"I will leave you two alone," Henri said to Amanda, "but I will be just inside should you need me. I will notify the pilot whenever you wish to make the return flight."

Valerie LaPalma gave the bodyguard a distracted wave as he passed, then focused on Amanda. "You were at the funeral," she said after scanning Amanda from head to toe. "And outside Mrs. Watkins's house, too, I believe."

Amanda was unnerved at the discovery of someone every bit as observant as she prided herself on being. "Yes. Thank you for agreeing to see me."

Valerie shrugged ruefully. "Did I really have a choice? Armand feels he knows what is best for everyone in his life. I'm no exception. Sometimes it is easier to give in than to argue."

"He denied at first knowing where you were. Why would he do that?"

"To give me the illusion that I had the right to refuse to see you. Trust me, though, there was never any doubt. He would not have called at all if he hadn't wished this meeting to take place." She looked Amanda over thoroughly once again, this time as if sizing her up. "He must hold you in very high regard."

"I would like to think he respects my journalistic ability."

Valerie laughed. "I doubt that your professional capabilities have much to do with it. You are quite lovely, and Armand admires great beauty above almost anything. It's his one failing."

Amanda was oddly disgruntled by the suggestion that Valerie LaPalma knew the workings of Armand's mind so intimately. Because their relationship was none of her business beyond its impact on this particular story, she forced herself to get to the heart of her reason for flying to France. "Ms. LaPalma, why are you here?"

"To recover from my friend's suicide," she said bluntly. "Isn't that obvious?"

"At the risk of offending you, you seem to me like a woman capable of overcoming anything you set your mind to—without running away."

Valerie's direct gaze faltered slightly. "You of all people should know that even the strongest women are not invincible."

"Meaning?"

"I'm familiar with your work, Ms. Roberts. By the way, can we cut the formality?"

"Of course."

"Good. You're a resourceful reporter, Amanda. Lord knows you make Gregory Fine quake in his boots."

Amanda was delighted to hear it. She barely resisted the urge to gloat. Fortunately Valerie didn't give her a chance. She was studying Amanda speculatively.

"You are a woman who is not afraid to take on anyone, regardless of their power, am I right?" she asked.

"I'd like to think so."

"But even you must have your moments of doubt, those times in the middle of the night when you fear reprisals, when you fear that justice might not triumph. What do you do then?"

Because she had asked as if Amanda's answer really mattered, Amanda tried to give her an honest reply. "I fight harder to remember why I got into this business."

"And that is?"

"Corny as it may sound, I wanted to make the world a

little better. Isn't that what motivated you to go to work for a senator?''

For some reason Amanda couldn't guess, Valerie looked pleased by her response. Her wary expression slipped away. She put aside her juice and removed her sunglasses, so that Amanda could read the sincerity in her eyes. The gesture could have been a studied attempt to disarm, but Amanda didn't think so.

''That's it exactly,'' Valerie agreed. ''And, dammit, I've done a good job of it, too. I've done some policy work on environmental issues and health care and the budget deficit that has already made a difference in the way we do things on Capitol Hill. I haven't had to compromise my integrity to do it, either.''

Amanda wasn't quite sure why Valerie was so vehement or what this had to do with Mary Allison. She decided to bring the conversation back on track. ''Did Mary Allison share your vision?''

Valerie sighed. ''Mary Allison was even better than I ever thought of being. She had a core of solid steel, but she tempered it with a sweetness and innocence that made people want to help her. Attila the Hun with a southern accent. I tend to cut to the chase too abruptly. I'm impatient. She knew how to woo a wavering senator into line. Perhaps that's why . . .'' Her voice trailed off.

''Why what?'' Amanda asked.

Valerie paused before replying, and Amanda couldn't help wondering if the silence was as calculated as the subtle hesitation purely to pique her interest.

"Perhaps that's why some people might have misinterpreted what she was all about," Valerie said.

It was yet another enigmatic response. Amanda had to temper her annoyance. "I don't understand."

"Capitol Hill is the last bastion of the good old boys," Valerie explained patiently as if it were a lesson in civics given to a slow pupil. "Many, though certainly not all, of the men think that their female colleagues are pure window dressing. They figure the women got elected as a backlash against the Anita Hill hearings. You would think that would have awakened them to the issue of sexual harassment, but a good many of them are still winking behind their hands like kids who've gotten away with sneaking a quickie behind the barn. If they feel that way about their fellow senators and representatives, just imagine how they feel about the women on their staffs."

Amanda was beginning to get an inkling of what Valerie was suggesting. As always when she finally zeroed in on the heart of a story, she felt a little thrill of excitement.

"Was Mary Allison being sexually harassed on the job?" she asked carefully. "Perhaps because people thought she was seducing them, not their votes?"

Valerie gazed at Amanda, her expression miserable and uncertain. "I'm not sure," she said softly.

"But you believe she was."

"I believe she *thought* she was."

"And the situation was so out of hand, so impossible for her, that she committed suicide," Amanda guessed.

"Perhaps. But I never would have thought in a hundred

years that Mary Allison would commit suicide. She was decent and strong. She wasn't a coward. She would have fought back.''

Amanda wanted to be absolutely certain what Valerie was suggesting, and she didn't want to put words in her mouth. "Fought back how?"

"I think she'd been tormented by the decision for months, but I think she was about to go public."

"And name names."

"One name."

"Who?"

Valerie slid her sunglasses back into place, allowing the suspense to build. Then, with a note of regret in her voice, she said, "Senator Rawlings."

Amanda's initial openmouthed astonishment died quickly. Vivid memories of the senator's earlier reaction to her comment that he seemed *fond* of Mary Allison made what Valerie was suggesting disgustingly plausible. Personally outraged by the possibility, she barely kept her feelings hidden as she said carefully, "She was going to accuse Blaine Rawlings publicly of sexual harassment? Was he aware of that?"

Valerie's expression turned bleak. "Absolutely."

CHAPTER

Seven

AMANDA'S head was reeling. As if it weren't enough that Valerie had flat-out accused Senator Blaine Rawlings of sexual harassment, Amanda concluded from her delicately phrased, enigmatic remarks that there was even a strong possibility he had murdered Mary Allison Watkins to keep her quiet. If Valerie suspected all this, no wonder she was hiding out.

Donelli's frequent warnings against jumping to conclusions quickly came to mind, but they were no match for this particular conclusion. It practically begged to be drawn from Valerie's subtle hints and innuendos. The fact that she instinctively distrusted all politicians didn't help. It did make her aware of the need to proceed with extreme caution.

As explosive as the sexual harassment allegations alone were, Amanda knew she had to prove them—or at least prove that Mary Allison had intended to level them—

before she could print them. And as everyone in the entire nation knew, thanks to Anita Hill, proving harassment was not going to be easy, especially with the alleged victim now dead. Maybe she could at least find substantiation of Mary Allison's intentions.

"She told you about the harassment?" she asked Valerie, hoping for some sort of confirmation she could actually publish. She needed to attribute the whole sordid tale to someone in a position to know what had been going on not only with Mary Allison, but behind closed doors in the senator's office.

"Never in so many words," she admitted. "But off and on now for months, she'd ask me if he ever made off-color comments to me, if he ever hinted around that he'd like me to make more than policy reports for him, that kind of thing."

"Had he?"

"I suppose so," she said.

"Suppose so?" Amanda repeated impatiently. This woman was definitely not a prosecutor's dream witness, much less a journalist's most reliable source. She had no backbone. "Either he did or he didn't."

Valerie scowled, as if she'd guessed Amanda's rapidly sinking opinion of her. "It wasn't that blatant," she explained. Suddenly she was no longer hesitant. She leaned forward. "Besides, you have to understand the difference between Mary Allison and me. I can give as good as I get from anybody. I'm not easily intimidated. It may not be very politically correct, but I can let that sort of stuff roll off my back, put a guy in his place with a snappy retort, and think nothing more about it. I have never, with Blaine Rawlings or anyone else, felt as if my job depended on putting up with something I personally found offensive. To me power is the distinction between kidding around and harassment, nothing more.''

''But doesn't the senator have the same power over you that he had over Mary Allison?''

''Bottom line? Of course he does. But power only works if the victim is afraid. I'm not. Mary Allison was. She thanked God every day for giving her the chance to work in Washington. She was terrified it would be taken away from her. I could get another job twenty minutes after leaving the senator's office. Mary Allison could have, too, but she never had the self-confidence to believe she could. He would have had her where he wanted her, and he would have known it. More important, *she* would have known it.''

She met Amanda's gaze evenly. ''If he was harassing her in the first place.''

Amanda had listened to more than Valerie's words. She'd listened to the underlying currents, the vague hint of doubt that had underscored every word. ''You don't think he was, do you?''

Valerie sighed with obvious regret. ''I told you before, I'm not certain. I think he might have said some things that she misinterpreted. Mary Allison was surprisingly naive, and he *is* on the chauvinistic side.'' She shook her head. ''More than that? I can't picture it. You've met him. Does he strike you as a dirty old man?''

Amanda thought of the image of southern charm and graciousness that was Blaine Rawlings's public trademark. She would have guessed Gregory Fine capable of harassment more readily than Rawlings, but that was personal bias as much as anything.

''No,'' she admitted, though her first instinct always was to believe the woman. For too many years their cries had been ignored. It made it difficult for any woman to risk her own reputation by making an accusation—no matter how well founded—that could backfire and destroy her, rather than the man she sought to expose.

''Would she lie, though?'' she asked Valerie. ''Nothing you or anyone else has told me about Mary Allison suggests that she was capable of manufacturing a charge like this or that she was stupid enough to do it, knowing the likely consequences.''

''I know,'' Valerie agreed. ''That's what makes this so confusing. I wish I knew what had been going on with her the last few weeks. She was so remote, possibly because she sensed I didn't really believe what she was hinting at.''

''There you go,'' Amanda said. ''That's my point exactly. You were her best friend, and you didn't believe her. Why would any woman deliberately set herself up for the kind of glaring spotlight that was bound to follow those kinds of accusations unless she was telling the truth? Why

would she even consider going public without documenta-
tion or witnesses or corroborating cases?''

''I can't answer that. One thing you should know,
though, if you don't already. Zack Downs and Senator
Rawlings can't stand each other. Zack hopes to be elected
to the Senate next time around. His specialty is foreign
affairs.''

Amanda grasped the implications at once. ''Meaning it
might be extremely helpful to a freshman senator if there
was a void in the foreign affairs leadership in the Senate?
If a scandal destroyed Senator Rawlings, it wouldn't break
the congressman's heart.''

''Exactly.''

Amanda considered that possibility, as well as the timing. A scandal only months before the election, even one
based on trumped-up charges, would be devastating to a
campaign. There wasn't sufficient time to disprove the
accusations. ''Innocent until proven guilty'' had little bear-
ing in the heat of a political race. Had Mary Allison been
an unwitting or a willing pawn in some scheme by Zachary
Downs?

''What you're suggesting doesn't speak very well of a
woman who was supposed to be your best friend.''

Tears welled up in Valerie's eyes then, and her stiff
demeanor crumpled. ''Don't you think I know that? I
don't like thinking that Zack could have manipulated Mary
Allison into planning those charges against the senator. I
don't like thinking that the charges were true. I sure as hell

don't like thinking that the man I've worked for for the past twelve years, a man I've believed in, is capable of sexual harassment, much less doing something to silence his accuser.''

Despite the tears, Amanda found she was surprisingly unsympathetic toward Valerie LaPalma. And she couldn't help wondering why a woman who'd described herself as tough and not easily intimidated would be hiding out in France if she thought even for an instant that her best friend had been killed to assure her silence. Shouldn't a woman like that be back home raising a ruckus to get at the truth? Or was she genuinely afraid that she knew or had guessed too much and might become another victim?

Amanda had a lot of time to think about that on the flight back to Washington. Thanks to the wonders of air travel and time zones, she was home by late afternoon, suffering from minimal jet lag and just in time to stop by Zachary Downs's office. She'd decided it was about time to get to know the bereaved senior representative from neighboring Alabama to find out just how shrewd and calculating he was capable of being.

Given his political aspirations, Zachary Taylor Downs had been conveniently named, though he claimed no kinship with the past president, from what Amanda had been able to learn over Armand's computer modem in the plane. She guessed from the cautious way Henri permitted her to use the modem that the hookup had astonishing capabilities to cull information from all sorts of normally unavailable sources. He discreetly gave her acccess to only one or two fairly ordinary data bases of biographical information and newspaper summaries. The uses to which Armand might put the more sophisticated aspects of the system weren't something she cared to explore too closely. She only wished the flight had been longer so she could have tapped into its resources on the senator and Greg Fine. She had a feeling that even with the limited access she'd been given, she would have learned more than Jenny Lee could possibly have sent along in those faxes back in her hotel room.

As for Downs, he had been born in rural Alabama, the grandson of poor but honest sharecroppers, according to his carefully slanted official bio. Amanda had to admit that reference to humble beginnings, even one generation removed, was a nice touch. It was only later, in another report, that she learned his parents had ascended from a sharecropper's cabin to a mansion by the time he came along.

He had played college football for Bear Bryant's Crimson Tide, earning himself national acclaim as an all-American and the kind of statewide popularity that boded well for a run for the state legislature a scant six years later. He'd run on a platform emphasizing education and economic reform, two issues of high priority in a state that had lagged behind in both.

Over the course of his first term, he'd made it evident that Montgomery was too provincial for the kinds of ideas he wanted to see become law. He set his sights on Washington, added a conservative foreign policy stance to his rousing speeches, and wound up on the steps of Capitol Hill by the time he was thirty-two. If Valerie LaPalma was correct about his ambition, he hoped to be a senator well before he turned forty.

At the moment, however, Zachary Taylor Downs was in a royal snit from what Amanda could observe from his outer office. She couldn't see the object of his ire, but from what she could hear—mostly loud, angry tones, not specific words—the individual clearly had failed in some task critical to the salvation of humanity at the very least. Surely nothing less would have deserved such a tirade.

Listening to him, Amanda decided she didn't like the man who, from all reports, had been the catch of Washington until he'd been snared by the supposedly fortunate Mary Allison Watkins. Nor could she reconcile the man throwing the irrational tantrum with the one Dee-Ann Watkins had described as stiff and formal.

Eventually a red-faced young woman emerged from the office, took one look at Amanda, and turned pale. Without sparing Amanda a second glance, she scooted through the door, then slammed it behind her in a belated gesture of defiance. Her departure left Amanda with the unsavory task of knocking on Downs's door without an intermediary to smooth her way.

Actually, though, the idea of letting him know his outburst had been overheard by a member of the media gave her a certain sense of satisfaction. She knocked with quite a bit of enthusiasm.

"What is it now, dammit? I thought I told you I didn't want to be disturbed."

Amanda took the snapped reply as an invitation. She poked her head in. "Mr. Downs?"

He glanced up, his expression fierce. "Who the hell are you?"

Amanda could hardly wait to tell him. She crossed the office, dropped her card on his desk, and waited for a reaction. She wasn't disappointed.

He muttered something. His complexion turned almost as pale as that of the hapless young woman who'd darted out moments earlier. Eyes the shade and warmth of granite met hers. The frosty look was barely tempered by an insincere smile that wouldn't have garnered many votes.

"Did we have an appointment?" he inquired testily.

"No. I'm afraid I took a chance that you might be available."

"Perhaps you should call my media liaison and arrange a time. I'm in the middle of something of a crisis right now."

"World peace, perhaps?" she inquired sweetly.

His head snapped up at that. "I've heard about you," he said in a way that implied she was meeting his low expectations.

She didn't waste time pretending to mistake his meaning. "Then doesn't it make sense to talk to me now and get me out of your hair?"

He drummed his fingers on his desk and studied her, his

expression still antagonistic. "Fine," he said eventually. "Let's start with what you're doing here."

It sounded as if he thought he was the one who got to do the interview. Rather than explaining, Amanda framed her reply in the form of a question, just to prove she knew how to seize control of a conversation as well as he did.

"Do you think Mary Allison committed suicide?" she inquired bluntly.

The question dropped through the already tense air like lead. His square chin set stubbornly, as if he'd determined not to answer such an absurd question. Amanda just sat back and outwaited him.

"Why are you trying to create doubt about something that has been established with certainty by the authorities?" he said eventually.

"Has it?" she retorted.

"If you're half as good as they say you are, you've read the reports. You know it has been."

"But were they pressured into making a snap judgment?"

"Is that an accusation, Ms. Roberts?"

She shook her head. "I could have sworn it was a question, a fairly direct one at that."

"Then I'll give you a direct answer. No, they were not pressured into making that finding." He paused. "At least not by me."

Amanda gathered he wanted her to suspect that others had pressured the police. Just to be clear on the point, she persisted, "Are you satisfied that everyone left the matter entirely in the hands of the police and the medical examiner?''

''What Senator Rawlings did is something you'll have to take up with him,'' he said

He said it a trifle smugly, it seemed to Amanda. ''I was thinking more of your senior staff people, who might have taken it upon themselves to urge swiftness in order to lessen your distress.''

He looked infuriated by the suggestion. ''My senior staff people do not take it upon themselves to do anything in my name,'' he retorted. ''Especially the sort of thing you're suggesting. I would fire them immediately.''

Perhaps he had done just that, Amanda thought, recalling the angry young woman who'd departed his office only moments before after being soundly chastised for something. She wondered if she would be back at work in the morning or, if not, if she could be tracked down and persuaded to reveal what her sin had been. With that ace up her sleeve, she decided it was time to make peace.

She smiled what she hoped he'd view as a conciliatory smile. ''Perhaps we should start over. I really am not here to make trouble. I simply want to do an in-depth profile of Mary Allison. I'm sure you know how highly regarded she was in Atlanta. Here was a young woman who had the job of her dreams, a young woman about to marry the man she loved, and she threw it all away. I know it must be painful for you to talk about, but do you have any idea why she would do that?''

''No, Ms. Roberts, I do not,'' he said curtly. ''Obviously it wasn't something she discussed with me, or she wouldn't have been in that car on that road that afternoon. I would have been with her, seeing that she got the help she needed."

Amanda ignored the sarcasm. "Had she been upset about something?"

He sighed heavily, and some of the antagonism seemed to ease out of him, to be replaced by raw pain. "That is something I have asked myself a hundred times a day since last Saturday."

His response was almost as believable as the senator's had been the day before. He leaned forward on his chair and regarded Amanda evenly, as if to reassure her that he was about to impart the truth, the whole truth, and nothing but the truth.

"I'm not the most observant man in the world. I'm a workaholic. Mary Allison understood that about me, which is why we got along so well. If she was troubled, either she hid it from me or I was just too damned blind to see it."

The last was uttered angrily and with a hint of self-loathing that could have been honest or merely a ploy to convince Amanda of his sincerity. Since she didn't trust politicians in general and this one in particular, she decided to put aside the matter of his honesty for the moment.

"Why did you ask her to marry you?"

He seemed taken aback by the question. "I loved her, of course."

Amanda persisted, wanting more than the obvious. "But if the newspapers are to be believed, you had your pick of any woman in Washington or Alabama. What was it about Mary Allison that drew you to her?"

He looked as if he'd never considered that before. He probably hadn't, Amanda thought cynically. He'd probably decided it was time to get married and chosen the first suitable woman to cross his path. He wouldn't be the first man to mistake expediency for love.

"You didn't know her, did you?" he said, surprising her with the genuine softening of his expression.

She shook her head.

"She was a lovely, gentle woman. We shared a common background. She knew who I was, what I was about, and she encouraged me." He gazed directly into Amanda's eyes, his own eyes suspiciously moist. "She was my strength, Ms. Roberts."

It was a pretty quotation, Amanda thought cynically. A touching act. It would play well in Georgia. She regarded him intently, trying to assess whether it had been based on sincere emotion. She honestly couldn't tell.

He had turned away to stare out the window. "If there's nothing further, I'd really like to be alone now."

To her surprise, the last sixty seconds had filled Amanda with a gut-wrenching uncertainty. She felt as if she'd just systematically pulled the wings off a fly that had previously seemed indestructible. At any rate with that one simple phrase, *"She was my strength,"* he had shaken all of her earlier impressions. Either Zack Downs was a master manipulator or he had genuinely loved the woman he had buried only forty-eight hours earlier.

As she walked slowly down the office building steps, Amanda wished like hell she could be certain exactly which he was. She also wondered whether Mary Allison had returned that love with such blind devotion that she would have intentionally set out to destroy a powerful senator who might stand in the way of her fiancé's political aspirations.

C H A P T E R

Eight

AMANDA had reached the street when she had the disquieting sense that she was being followed. It was past rush hour, and the streets were practically deserted. Hearing the hurried footsteps behind her made her pulse leap. She knew all about crime statistics in the nation's capital. Violent incidents were disproportionately high and the subject of constant study by the media and dismay from public officials.

She picked up her pace. She caught sight of a taxi in the next block and was just about to make a run toward it when she heard her name called out by a hesitant and vaguely familiar feminine voice.

"Ms. Roberts?"

Amanda stopped and turned, then spotted the receptionist she'd met the day before in Blaine Rawlings's office, hurrying to catch up with her. Her movements were slowed by her high heels and straight skirt.

"Do you have a minute?" Ms. Wilcox asked. She brushed her windblown hair from her face and regarded Amanda with evident nervousness. "There's something I'd like to talk to you about."

As exhausted as she was from the overseas flight and the draining encounter with Zack Downs, Amanda never turned down the chance to listen when someone was in the mood to spill their guts, especially when she'd previously gotten the impression that that same person was withholding something.

"Sure. Is there someplace nearby where we can get a cup of coffee?" She figured she'd need the caffeine to keep her eyes open, unless the receptionist's revelations were particularly startling.

The woman shook her head, glancing around nervously. "I mean, there is, but it would be better if I weren't seen with you. We've been given strict instructions by Mr. Fine not to talk to reporters. Around this neighborhood somebody's bound to spot us."

Amanda nodded, delighted with the prospect of defying one of Greg Fine's orders. "Let's take a cab to my hotel, then. Would that be all right?"

Ms. Wilcox still looked uncertain, but apparently she couldn't come up with a viable alternative. She followed Amanda into the street, where Amanda hailed a cab with the experience of a former New Yorker.

At the hotel, her reluctant source insisted they go upstairs. She paced Amanda's room from one side to the other while they waited for room service to deliver coffee.

The knock on the room's door sent Amanda's guest scurrying into the bathroom. Obviously this was not a woman used to secret assignations.

Hoping to reassure her, Amanda tried desperately to recall the complete nameplate on the woman's desk. She remembered Wilcox, but she wanted to get onto a first-name basis. Had it been Patricia?

"The coffee's here," she announced cheerfully, drawing the woman back into the room. She handed her a cup and smiled. "It's Patricia, isn't it?"

The woman's nod seemed almost automatic, but her expression said she was reluctant to confirm it. She gazed at Amanda's tape recorder worriedly.

"I won't turn it on unless you tell me it's okay," she reassured her. "I would like to know your name, though. I remember Wilcox. I'm just not sure about your first name."

"It's Patricia . . . Patricia Wilcox," she said finally, sitting on the edge of a chair and balancing the coffee cup on her knee. "You won't publish it or anything, will you?"

"Not without your permission."

"I'm sorry if I seemed rude yesterday. It's just that things have been in such a state lately." Her expression hardened. "I blame Mary Allison for that," she said, and then immediately looked miserable.

"And you feel guilty about blaming her, because she's dead," Amanda guessed.

Ms. Wilcox sighed with relief. "That's it exactly."

"What do you blame Mary Allison for?"

"Everyone being so on edge."

"Do you know why? Was it something she'd done? Something she was going to do?"

"I'm not supposed to know this, you see," Ms. Wilcox said conspiratorially. "I mean, it's not something she would have told me. We weren't close or anything. And obviously it's not something the senator would want spread around, if you know what I mean."

At this rate, it was going to take her hours to get to the point. Amanda decided to help her along, even if it meant putting words in her mouth. "You'd heard she was going to accuse him of sexual harassment, hadn't you?"

Patricia Wilcox's already troubled blue eyes widened with shock. "You know?"

Amanda nodded. "How did you feel when you heard about it?"

"You mean did I believe it? No, absolutely not. That's why I had to come to see you. You can destroy the senator by printing these lies. There's not a finer gentleman in all of Washington than Senator Rawlings. When my little girl got sick several years ago, he came all the way down to my house in Woodbridge, Virginia, to see her. It was on a Sunday afternoon. He brought her a beautiful doll, too. Does that sound like the kind of man who'd mistreat the women on his staff?" she demanded indignantly.

Amanda declined to comment on that. Serial killer Ted Bundy had charmed everyone around him, and look what he had done. She pursued the senator's behavior in the office instead. "He's never said or done anything around you that made you the least bit uncomfortable?"

"Never! I am in and out of that office all day long. If he was the kind to make off-color suggestions, he'd have plenty of opportunities, but he's always polite as can be. The most personal thing he's ever said to me was asking about my little girl."

Patricia Wilcox was an attractive, middle-aged woman, but she wasn't in the same league as Mary Allison Watkins. Perhaps the senator simply hadn't been interested in her. "Have you ever overheard him say anything suggestive to another female member of his staff?"

"Not once."

"Does he automatically close the door to his office when women are in there?"

"He closes it when anyone's in there for an important meeting."

"You said you weren't particularly close to Mary Allison. What about the other women on the senator's staff? Do you know them well?"

"There's Carla Boggs. She's Mr. Fine's secretary. She and I have lunch together sometimes."

"Has she ever suggested that she's been approached by the senator?"

A genuine smile finally broke across Patricia Wilcox's previously tense features. "Carla's a sixty-two-year-old black woman who weighs about two hundred pounds. She could probably wallop him clear back to Georgia. I doubt she has a problem with anybody on the Hill."

"So you've never heard anything from anyone that would corroborate Mary Allison's accusations? Never seen Senator Rawlings patting a woman on the fanny or grabbing at one, no matter how innocent it all seemed?"

"Never. You have to believe he would never do something like that. I mean, he doesn't even joke around the way some of the other men do. I've heard what they say to their secretaries. It makes all those accusations against Clarence Thomas seem downright silly. No wonder that committee didn't see what the big deal was."

So Patricia Wilcox had never personally been harassed by Blaine Rawlings. Amanda knew from her own experience early in her career that sexual harassment was not always equitably distributed among all the women in an office. That didn't mean it didn't occur or that a pattern couldn't be found if enough women were questioned. In her case, a sleazy city editor on a suburban paper had hit only on starting reporters too naive and too lacking in self-confidence to fight back. They'd needed him as a reference if their careers had any hope of a future. Patricia Wilcox's vehement defense of the senator was the truth as she knew it. Valerie LaPalma had a similar view. Even with two against one, that didn't mean that Mary Allison hadn't been a victim.

With a sense of resignation, Amanda realized she'd have to start questioning all of the senator's women staffers, past and present, before she could be sure of anything. Even then the answer might fall into a gray area between guilt and innocence. The prospect was daunting, especially given her rapidly approaching deadline.

"Was the senator aware that Mary Allison might file charges?" she asked now. That would certainly explain the defensiveness in his tone when she'd questioned him about his fondness for the woman. It would also explain why Greg Fine had ordered his staff to refuse to speak with reporters.

"I think so. Gregory, I mean Mr. Fine, he certainly knew. I doubt he would have kept a thing like that from Senator Rawlings."

"Do you have any idea how Mr. Fine found out? Did Mary Allison tell him? Or had he heard it from somebody else, maybe another staffer she had taken into her confidence?"

"I don't know. I overheard Mr. Fine talking about it on the phone, but it sounded as if he already knew, not like he was just being told."

"Had anyone confronted Mary Allison about her plans?"

She shook her head. "This all happened last Friday, the day before she died. I think Mr. Fine was planning to talk to her this week. He'd asked me to set up an appointment for the two of them on Monday. If I'd seen her, I'd have told her a thing or two myself."

"Why did you schedule the appointment and not Ms. Boggs?"

"Carla was out sick all last week. Anyway, he blocked

out two hours. Usually he has appointments scheduled every fifteen minutes or so. That's why I knew this was really important. It had to be about the harassment, don't you think? Gregory was going to stop her before she ruined that fine man.''

It didn't really matter what Amanda thought. The only thing that mattered was that Mary Allison's threats had apparently stirred up a real commotion, and before it could be resolved, she had died. Correction. Before it could be *discussed,* she had died. Her death had certainly resolved things for the senator. His reputation—for the moment, at least—remained unblemished.

Amanda wanted in the worst way to pin Mary Allison's death on the overly zealous Gregory Fine. She could just see the sleazy little man taking it upon himself to rid the senator of a problem by killing Mary Allison with no more compassion than he'd display swatting a fly. She could also see him being smart enough to put an appointment with her on his calendar for the following week to divert suspicion. Unfortunately, objective reporters couldn't allow their personal dislikes to get in the way of impartial reporting. She was going to have to interview Gregory Fine with an open mind and a civil tongue. God help her.

But first she was going to go through every single one of the faxes Jenny Lee had sent so that she would know exactly the sort of person she was up against.

As soon as Patricia Wilcox had departed amid a flurry

of pleas for Amanda to drop the story, Amanda ordered a sandwich from room service and pulled out the files. There were at least a dozen profiles of the senator included, most of them from the *Atlanta Journal-Constitution*, one from *The Washington Post*, one from *The New York Times*, and one from a competing Atlanta magazine. She put those aside for the moment and picked up the faxed articles mentioning Gregory Fine. There was precious little information in them. In every one of them he was mentioned only in terms of his work for the senator. Chief of Staff Gregory Fine reported this. Gregory Fine commented on that.

Amanda reached for the phone and called *Inside Atlanta*. "Hey, Jenny Lee," she said, automatically falling into the southern accent that was beginning to creep into her voice more and more. She needed a long trip home to New York soon, she decided as she listened to herself.

"Amanda, hon, where have you been? Oscar's about to flip a gizzard. He's left half a dozen messages for you just since lunchtime."

"Sorry. I had to go to France. Then I was up on Capitol Hill. I just got back and haven't picked up my messages yet."

"France! You went to France? Does Joe know? I thought you were working a story in Washington. Amanda, does this have anything to do with Armand? You aren't cheating on Joe, are you?"

"Hey, slow down. I did go on Armand's plane, but he

stayed right here. I had to get to a source, and it turned out she was in France. I think Joe knows, since he and Armand have been chatting regularly about my safety.''

"Oh, my," Jenny Lee said, the wind obviously having been stripped from her sails. "What is Oscar going to say?"

"Oscar is going to be very pleased that I got to Valerie LaPalma," Amanda assured her. "Was he calling for any particular reason or just to check up on my whereabouts?"

Before Jenny Lee could answer, Amanda heard Oscar.

"Is that her? Is that Amanda? I'm going to kill her. Give me that phone."

Amanda considered disconnecting the line but figured that would only delay the inevitable. "Hi, Oscar."

"Would you mind explaining to me why I've had three calls today from Washington suggesting that my overly zealous reporter ought to be horse-whipped and that if I didn't see to it that she was, there were others willing to do the job for me? I believe Joel has had similar calls."

As the magazine's publisher, Joel Crenshaw was never intimidated by official queries. In fact, out of respect for Amanda's journalistic skills, he was even better than Oscar at telling such callers to take a hike. The fact that everyone had gone running to him suggested there was a lot of desperation in the nation's capital. Amanda was pleased.

"Let me guess," she said cheerfully. "Senator Rawlings. Gregory Fine. And Congressman Downs."

"At least you're keeping track of whom you've offended. I thought we discussed a discreet investigation,

Amanda. At this rate, the president himself will know what you're up to by morning.''

"Maybe he should know that one of his party's most prominent senators was about to be charged with sexual harassment by a woman who is now dead, a woman whose death occurred under very mysterious circumstances.''

Oscar sucked in his breath. "That's what you've been saying? No wonder everyone's in such a state. What are you trying to do, shut this magazine down?''

"It's not what I've been saying,'' she explained patiently. "It's what I've been hearing. So far, though, I don't have absolute proof that Mary Allison intended to make those charges. Nor have I found anyone else who'll make the same claims against Senator Rawlings. Now can I speak to Jenny Lee again? I need her to do some research for me tonight.''

The request was greeted with dead silence.

"Oh, Oscar, are you there?''

"I'm in shock. What's he supposed to have done? Told her she had a great tush? Is that a crime? Chased her around his desk? Okay, she could probably outrun him anyway. Ordered her into his bed? Can you see Blaine Rawlings doing that?''

"He wouldn't be the first man to consider any of that to be business as usual,'' Amanda reminded her boss. "And, yes, by the way, telling her she has a great tush is a crime, unless he's a physician dealing with medical facts.''

"Jesus, Amanda, the next thing you know a man's not

going to be able to open his mouth without getting slapped with a sexual harassment suit.''

"He's not, unless he cleans up what comes out," she agreed. "Come on, Oscar. You know you'd never say anything like that to me or to Jenny Lee."

"I suppose not," he conceded with obvious reluctance. He sometimes hated not being on the side of the good ole boys. Unfortunately, a career in journalism and contact with Amanda had made him more politically correct than some of his buddies. "You gonna be able to nail something down by deadline?"

"If you'll put Jenny Lee on the line, I might have a shot at it."

"Okay, okay. I'll tell Joel what's going on," he promised. "And, Amanda, if it's true, you get the son of a bitch, okay?"

She grinned. He'd come through for her again. "You bet. I can't wait, in fact."

When Jenny Lee got back on the line, Amanda asked her to do a thorough check on Gregory Fine. "I want to know if the man has so much as a parking violation against him."

"Why? I thought you were going after Rawlings."

"The senator might have been guilty of sexual harassment, but I think Greg Fine is capable of committing murder to cover it up."

CHAPTER
Nine

JENNY Lee woke Amanda out of a sound sleep at dawn on Friday.

"You're not going to believe this," she announced, her voice filled with excitement.

Amanda felt as if she'd been dragged across a continent, feet first. Her head was pounding. "Without coffee, I'm not going to believe anything. What time is it?"

"Almost seven."

"In which time zone?"

"Amanda, honey, what's wrong with you? You're usually the one who's wide awake first thing in the morning."

"And you're usually dead to the world," she retorted, seriously considering drinking the cold coffee left in the pot from the night before. Hot or cold, caffeine was caffeine, right? "Did you stay up all night?"

"Just about. I called Joe, by the way. He did a little

checking on those data bases he has, too. He called me back a little while ago. Said to tell you he loved you and to hurry home."

"Was that in the data base?" Amanda inquired crankily, wondering why he hadn't called her himself to tell her that. He was probably too anxious to get out to those damned fields of his. Or maybe now that he'd passed her off to Armand for protection, he figured he didn't need daily contact to relieve his mind. "Okay, I'm awake. What did you find?"

"Your Mr. Gregory Fine graduated summa cum laude from Harvard. He was top of his class in law school. He started his career in one of New York's biggest law firms, married a genuine debutante." As a former debutante herself, Jenny Lee managed to make the latter sound like his greatest accomplishment.

"So far, you're not making my day," Amanda commented. "I was hoping for sleaze. You're giving me sainthood."

"Hold your horses. I'm just getting to the good stuff. Ten years ago he left Batten, Davis, Patterson and Klein. His departure was requested. The reason for it was very hush-hush, but there was some suggestion that he'd been involved in insider trading, that he'd fed a few tips to a buddy at *The Wall Street Journal* and maybe to some selected associates at the same time."

"But he wasn't charged?"

"Nope. Not so much as a whiff of this ever came out. I'm sure *The Wall Street Journal* would have been just as anxious as Mr. Fine to keep things quiet. I had to call in some favors from some people in New York to get the whole story, once I discovered he'd left that law firm under some sort of ol' cloud.''

''Even so, how'd he keep it quiet enough that Senator Rawlings didn't find out when he hired him? If you discovered it, surely the senator could have.''

''My one friend, who's at a competing law firm, says the rumor at the time was that the senator was one of the beneficiaries of said inside information. Supposedly he got the news one day ahead of the paper. Naturally it was in his best interests to hire Mr. Fine and keep the whole thing in the family.''

''Which means that Greg would in turn be very loyal to the senator now,'' Amanda deduced.

''Or that he'd always have something to hold over the senator's head,'' Jenny Lee countered.

''That would certainly shift the balance of power in the office,'' Amanda agreed thoughtfully. ''What happened to his wife? I thought he was single. I've never seen him with her or anyone else, for that matter. He's usually dogging the senator's footsteps all by his lonesome.''

''Since her daddy was a partner in the law firm, apparently she decided to cut Greg loose, just like Daddy did.''

Fascinating, Amanda thought. Suddenly she had a whole new perspective on how far Gregory Fine would go to make it to the top. One thing for sure, he would understand all about leverage when she tried to persuade him to tell what he knew.

* * *

Strolling into the senator's offices several hours later at midmorning, Amanda was careful to ignore Patricia Wilcox and head directly for the woman who had to be the indomitable Carla Boggs. Amanda was delighted to have the chance to meet her in person.

Mrs. Boggs was exactly as Patricia Wilcox had described her. She wore basic black, as if that might play down her size. It didn't help. She was every bit as intimidating as some hulking right tackle on the front line of the Atlanta Falcons. Not only physically capable of blocking the entryway to Gregory Fine's office, she had a way of looking at an interloper that immediately reminded Amanda of the way she'd felt in grade school when the principal had caught her in the hall without a pass. She slid her business card onto the desk by way of an introduction.

"I don't see an appointment down here for you," Mrs. Boggs announced, her gaze narrowed suspiciously.

As if that were news, Amanda thought. "I realize that," she said, barely restraining the childhood impulse to slink guiltily away. She mustered up her most confident smile. "I also know that you're the one person who can sneak me in to see him for a few minutes."

Dark brown eyes studied her. "Just why would I want to do that?"

Amanda got the impression that a sharp sense of humor lurked behind that austere facade. "Because you know Mr. Fine would want an opportunity to set the record straight on some very important issues before they're published in the senator's home state.''

"That don't mean you get to waltz in here without an appointment. Mr. Fine's a busy man. And this office has a media coordinator who likes to arrange the interviews. He wouldn't like me doing his job for him.''

"It's not exactly an interview. More like follow-up.''

"There's a difference?''

"If it'll get me through that door, there's a big difference.''

Grinning now, Mrs. Boggs studied Greg Fine's calendar. "Nope. Not a blessed minute the whole day long,'' she said firmly, then looked at Amanda, waiting for her next move. Apparently it was a game she enjoyed playing.

"Fifteen minutes,'' Amanda bargained. She glanced at the package of cream-filled pastries on Mrs. Bogg's desk. "And a week's supply of Twinkies.''

Mrs. Boggs chuckled. "Okay. I'll get you five,'' she retorted, and jotted a note on Gregory Fine's calendar. "You'll have to wait, though. He's in with the senator now.''

"How long?''

"You got someplace more important you gotta be?''

Amanda laughed, liking this blunt woman more by the minute and wondering how on earth she tolerated a weasel like Greg Fine. It was a question she'd have to ask later. She didn't want to risk offending her before she got through that door. For all she knew, Carla Boggs felt some deep, maternal bond with her boss.

"Well?" Mrs. Boggs demanded. "You in a hurry to get someplace else?"

Amanda had thought her question was rhetorical. "Nope," she admitted belatedly. "This is the only place on my agenda for this morning."

Mrs. Boggs nodded in satisfaction and went back to her typing. She glanced up a minute later. "You want a cup of coffee, there's some in that little room over there. I don't wait on nobody 'round here."

"Could I bring you back a cup?" Amanda asked.

"That'd be nice," she said, handing over her mug. It had her name on it, along with a picture of Mickey Mouse. "Won't get you inside any faster, though."

"I never thought it would."

Two cups of coffee and a half hour later, Carla Boggs buzzed Gregory Fine's office. How she'd guessed he was back in there, Amanda couldn't imagine. He'd never passed through the reception area and the door to his office had remained firmly shut. For all Amanda knew, he could have been there all along.

"You can go in now. Five minutes, remember. I don't want this schedule of mine thrown off the rest of the day."

"In and out," Amanda promised as she eased inside Greg Fine's office before Mrs. Boggs could change her mind and chase her off. Besides, once this meeting with Fine was over with, she wanted a chance to have a nice friendly chat with the woman about what she knew about the senator's behavior behind closed doors. Amanda had a feeling nothing escaped Carla Boggs's notice.

For the moment, though, she had to make the most of the five minutes she'd been allotted with the senator's chief of staff.

"What brings you back here?" Fine asked testily. "I thought we'd answered all your questions the other day."

"Something's come to my attention since then. I thought you might want to clarify it for me."

"I don't even want to talk to you."

"I can imagine," Amanda muttered.

"What's that?"

"I just said that it doesn't surprise me that you'd want to steer as far away from the media as possible."

He regarded her suspiciously. "Oh?"

"Given what happened at Batten, Davis, Patterson and Klein."

He scowled, but that was the full extent of his reaction. Amanda was disappointed. She'd hoped to have him quaking in his Italian leather loafers.

"If you have a point, get to it."

"Certainly. I've been made aware of certain allegations that Mary Allison Watkins was planning to make about Senator Rawlings."

That accomplished what her mention of the law firm had not. All of a sudden Gregory Fine's expensive silk tie seemed to be choking him. He ran a finger around his collar, then loosened the tie. It didn't help. His face was still beet red. "What allegations were those?" he asked.

Because he clearly didn't want to confirm anything until he was certain exactly how much she knew, Amanda cheerfully spelled it out. "She planned to charge that he had sexually harassed her."

"She told you that?" he inquired, a smirk of satisfaction replacing his stunned expression.

Amanda didn't like what that smirk implied about who currently had the upper hand. "No, but—"

"Surely you don't intend to put words into the mouth of a dead woman," he said.

"Not in print," she agreed, then made another stab at reclaiming the upper hand. "Not quite yet, anyway. That doesn't mean I won't explore the charges as a possible motive for murder."

CHAPTER

Ten

GREGORY Fine looked as if he'd swallowed something raw and distasteful, something he anticipated might be deadly. His sputters turned to racking coughs.

"Water?" Amanda offered pleasantly.

He glared at her. "Ms. Roberts, you repeat any of that hogwash about harassment and this office will sue you for slander. Print it and we'll sue for libel, and by God, we'll win."

"I'm not exactly sure what it is you think I've said," she said innocently. "I merely indicated that something like threatened exposure of sexual harassment might be considered a motive for murder. If you made some assumptions based on that, you can hardly hold me accountable."

"Don't you dare play word games with me," he snapped. "We both know what you were getting at."

Amanda lost patience as well. "What I'm getting at, Mr. Fine, is an understanding of why Mary Allison Watkins might have killed herself only hours after she'd picked out her wedding dress. Since that doesn't seem to add up as rational behavior, I'm looking for other explanations for her death. This one happened to fall into my lap."

"You'll never prove it was anything other than a suicide," he said smugly. "And suicide can hardly be considered a rational act under any circumstances. Totally sane people don't do it. Who's to say what might drive a woman to commit suicide? It could have been a split-second decision resulting from some real or imagined paranoia."

"Yesterday you told me she must have been despondent."

He waved off the apparently contradictory explanations. "I'm not a psychiatrist. I have no idea what her problem was. But I do believe she killed herself on that highway. So does everyone else who counts."

"Her mother doesn't."

"I'm talking about officials. The case has been closed. All of the police and medical reports are in."

"Oh, I daresay I can get it reopened if I come up with one or two people who might have had very good reasons to want that young woman dead." She decided not to mention that she already had one very smart Atlanta police detective digging around in the case, albeit unofficially.

His gaze narrowed. "Be careful, Ms. Roberts. Remember what happened last time you tried to cross the senator."

"Are you referring to the fact that the magazine and I

made a responsible decision to delay publication on a story until we were certain it would not harm a government operation?'' she inquired.

Even at the time, Amanda had known that decision was going to come back to haunt them. People like Greg Fine would see their actions as a weakness. He just didn't get what the role of the media was in a free society—to observe and report, to comment, not to recklessly endanger lives. At his smug nod, she decided to give him a short lesson on the subject.

''I think that's very different from a conspiracy to cover up wrongdoing by a United States senator by resorting to murder, don't you?''

''You're walking that line again,'' he warned.

Amanda forced herself to calm down. Trading insults wasn't getting her anywhere. She moderated her tone. ''Look, Mr. Fine, whether you believe me or not, I assure you that I am not out to get the senator. I'm after the truth. You could help me with that. If these charges are totally outrageous, then don't just throw up roadblocks to my investigation. Help me to establish the truth.''

''I'm telling you the truth.''

She shook her head at the sanctimonious statement. ''Sorry. I'm afraid your word alone isn't enough in this instance. Arrange for me to talk to the women on the senator's staff. Let me see if anyone can corroborate Mary Allison's charges.''

He regarded her suspiciously. ''That's all it will take to get you to back off?''

"If there's no corroborating evidence, there's no story," she assured him.

To her astonishment, he honestly seemed to be weighing the alternatives.

"I'll speak to Carla," he said finally. "She'll arrange for you to speak to anyone you like on the senator's staff. I'll see to it that everyone is told to give you their whole-hearted assistance."

Now it was Amanda's turn to choke. She had never expected complete access, much less such a high level of cooperation. Was it possible that Gregory Fine's initially hostile reaction had merely been a knee-jerk attempt to protect his boss from unjust accusations? Surely he wouldn't be this willing to assist her with setting up interviews if he thought for one instant that someone on staff could confirm Mary Allison's allegations. For the first time, she began to wonder if she was on the wrong track. The only way to find out would be to go through with each and every one of those interviews.

Now, as if to prove his good intentions, Fine buzzed his secretary and told her to assist Amanda in any way she could. "I want this settled as quickly as possible. We can't run a campaign with a cloud like this hanging over us."

"Thank you," Amanda said as she headed for the outer office. She couldn't help thinking that Gregory Fine's turn-around was a little too quick, a little too convenient, even if campaign expediency was at stake. Until the door to Fine's office was closed behind her, she kept waiting for a knife to hit her in the back. When she arrived at Carla Boggs's desk unscathed, she had to admit she felt a moment's disappointment.

"I don't have time to be settin' up appointments for you," Mrs. Boggs informed her. She held out a list of staffers, complete with their office extensions as well as their home addresses and phone numbers. "You're on your own. Just don't go keeping these people from their work. We don't have a lot of time to waste in this office, unlike some people who take civil service jobs as a license to steal from the government."

"I'll keep that in mind. And thank you. I appreciate your getting me in to see Mr. Fine," Amanda said.

She was almost to the door when she was struck by a sudden thought. What if other women who had been victimized had simply quit? She turned back. "Mrs. Boggs, what's turnover like around here?"

"You mean are folks quitting right and left?"

"Yes."

"No, ma'am. The senator believes in doling out responsibilities and then giving his people the freedom to do the job. It's a good place to work, decent salaries, good benefits, a nice pension. I'd say the people here count themselves lucky." She paused. "Of course, that's not to say we don't get a few with some ambition that use this place as a stepping-stone. We've had our share of those."

"Would you say you see more men or women like that?"

Mrs. Boggs's expression turned canny. "You're not foolin' me, young lady. I know what you're sniffin' around here for."

Amanda didn't doubt that for an instant. If Patricia Wilcox knew, then the even wiser Carla Boggs would know all about the sexual harassment accusations. "Am I going to find it?"

"No, ma'am, you're not, but I suppose my word's not going to be enough to convince you, is it?"

Amanda shook her head, even though the evidence was beginning to mount up against Mary Allison's claims. "I'm afraid not, but it's not because I don't believe you. It's just that I can't afford to overlook anything."

"How come you haven't asked me straight out about Mary Allison killing herself?"

Amanda loved interviewing people who were one step ahead of her. It saved time. "I was just getting to that, but my guess is you think it was suicide just like everybody else around here."

"Just shows what you know," Carla Boggs retorted. "If that girl killed herself, my name ain't Carla Louise Boggs. Somebody had a finger in her death, you can bet on that, but if you ask me, you're sniffin' in the wrong barnyard."

"Meaning?"

"You're smart enough. You figure it out."

Amanda took the list she'd gotten from Gregory Fine's office back to the hotel with her and began making notes on the people she needed to contact. There were only half a dozen besides the three women she'd already spoken with—Valerie LaPalma, Patricia Wilcox, and Carla Boggs. All except Valerie were secretaries or clerks. That didn't surprise her. Men still dominated the positions of responsibility on the Hill.

She realized that she'd have to make the calls or visits in the evening. Most women who had been harassed were not likely to be very forthcoming if the interview was being held under the watchful eye of their employer. Add to that Mrs. Boggs's warning about the workload. And the fact that face-to-face questioning was always better than phoning, which would allow the person to lie more easily without her being able to detect it.

Unfortunately, the women on the list were scattered. One lived in Georgetown, two lived in Bethesda, and the remaining three lived in Virginia—one in old Alexandria, one in a high-rise enclave near National Airport called Crystal City, and the other much farther west in Middleburg. Getting to them wasn't going to be easy, especially over a holiday weekend. It might not even make any sense to stay in town.

She debated going back to Atlanta, then decided that she'd spend the rest of the evening and early Saturday attempting contacts. If none panned out, she'd consider it an omen and go work the story from the Georgia angle for a few days. Then she'd make a fresh start in Washington after the holiday.

In the meantime, she'd need a rental car to get around

to spots she couldn't reach on the Metro. She called the desk and made arrangements. Just as she was hanging up, the phone rang again.

"Damn, Amanda, you're harder to find than some of these murder suspects I'm tracking," Jim Harrison said by way of a greeting when Amanda picked up.

"You know how I love to test your skills," she retorted as anticipation made her pulse speed up. "You must have something or you wouldn't have worked quite so hard to find me, much less spent department money to call long distance. You'd have left a message with somebody in Atlanta."

"Oh, I don't know," he taunted. "Perhaps I just wanted to rub it in. Spending a couple of bucks would be worth it to hear you eat crow."

"Are you saying that there was nothing suspicious about Mary Allison's car?" she asked, not bothering to keep the disappointment out of her voice.

"Stop trying to anticipate me. If you'll hush up a minute, I'll tell you what I found out."

"My lips are sealed."

He hooted at that. "Yeah, right. That would be a first. Anyway, the car's in the impound lot. I went over myself and had a look. From what I could tell, the mechanics were on the money about the brakes and stuff. Had one of the guys go over it with me just to confirm what I was seeing. That car was in tip-top mechanical shape."

"What about the paint?"

"Told you you couldn't keep quiet," he gloated.

"Detective!"

"All right, all right. I'm getting to it. The front end of that sucker is crumpled up like an accordion with all the air squeezed out of it. Most of the green paint job is probably still out there on that tree she hit."

He paused dramatically, evidently enjoying his moment in the limelight. Or, more likely, thoroughly enjoying Amanda's mounting frustration.

"Okay, Detective, we all agree you're a regular tease," she said irritably. "Get to the bottom line."

"As I said, the car's paint job is a real mess. But unless that tree was lined with silver, something else hit the left front fender."

So, Amanda thought gleefully, Dee-Ann Watkins had been right. "At the very least, what we're talking about here is a hit-and-run, right?"

"At the very least," he agreed, his voice suddenly somber. "At the worst? Somebody deliberately ran her off that road."

"Have you told the sheriff? Isn't that enough to get the case reopened?"

"I've kept this under my hat. Took a few pictures, just to make sure nobody paints over that sucker, then says I've made the whole thing up."

"Who might do that?"

"Well, it occurs to me that the sheriff might have had some motivation for not noticing that paint. The mechanic sure looked downright stunned when I pointed it out."

"You think the original inspectors, maybe even the

sheriff, could have been bribed, perhaps by a well-placed public official?''

''I'm just saying that anyone looking that car over from stem to stern could not have missed that paint or its implications,'' the detective said emphatically.

Amanda just loved conspiracies. They made reporting so much more fun. One involving local law enforcement and the U.S. Congress practically gave her palpitations.

C H A P T E R

Eleven

AS soon as she'd hung up, Amanda reconsidered whether she'd be more productive at home or in Washington over Labor Day. Five minutes later she was packing her bag. She wanted personally to survey the car rental agencies in Atlanta to determine if any of them had rented out a silver car that had been returned in less than perfect condition. Or perhaps had had a car kept out longer than originally anticipated, long enough for repairs to be completed. It wouldn't hurt to start checking body shops around town, either.

To accomplish all that, she was going to need help. She decided to wait until she was on the flight to Atlanta before phoning the office and getting Jenny Lee involved. In the meantime she had just enough time before her flight to stop by Crystal City and interview Leslie Baldwin, one of the women who worked in Senator Rawlings's office.

According to Mrs. Boggs's notation, she worked an early shift and ought to be home just about now.

Amanda cancelled her order for a rental car and opted for a taxi. In midafternoon, an hour or so before the start of rush-hour mayhem, it took less than twenty minutes to cross the Fourteenth Street Bridge to Virginia and get to the high rise listed on Mrs. Boggs's personnel roster.

There was a hotel-style reception desk to the left in the elegant marble lobby. Since that desk stood between her and the elevators, Amanda guessed it wasn't just for show. She approached the guard on duty.

"I'm here to see Leslie Baldwin."

"Your name?"

Amanda didn't think her name or her affiliation was likely to get her upstairs, not even after Gregory Fine's assurances that everyone on staff would be told to cooperate. An impersonal call from the security guard wasn't likely to accomplish it, either. She needed to talk to Ms. Baldwin directly.

She gave the guard, who looked to be Pakistani, her most persuasive smile. "She doesn't know me. Would it be possible for me to speak to her? I can explain who I am."

"That would be most irregular."

Amanda guessed he was worried she would lie about Ms. Baldwin's willingness to see her. "I'll have her speak to you before you admit me, so that you'll know it's all right."

He nodded reluctantly. "Yes. I can see how that would work." He dialed the intercom extension and handed Amanda the phone. To her relief, Leslie Baldwin picked up almost immediately.

Amanda introduced herself. "I need a few minutes of your time for the story I'm doing on Mary Allison Watkins."

"I know what you're after. Sleaze. Well, I won't be a party to it and that's final."

"Please, Ms. Baldwin. I swear to you that I'm not looking for tabloid-style sensationalism, just an honest profile."

"I can't talk now," she said in a way that didn't give any indication whether she believed Amanda's explanation. At least she hadn't slammed down the phone. "A friend is picking me up to go to Ocean City for the weekend. I thought it was him downstairs."

Amanda glanced around the lobby. There was a seating area off to one side. It was empty. It would be private enough to conduct an interview.

"Couldn't you bring your bag down and wait for him here? I promise we'll cut it short the minute he arrives. I have a plane to catch back to Atlanta myself."

Whether it was because she sensed she wouldn't have more than a moment or two alone with Amanda for questioning or because she was beginning to relent, Ms. Baldwin agreed to join Amanda in the lobby. She emerged from the elevator not five minutes later, rolling one large bag and carrying another over her shoulder. Obviously she didn't know the first thing about packing light. Amanda wondered what she took along on a real vacation.

As Leslie Baldwin crossed the lobby, Amanda studied her. Like so many young women who flocked to Washington hoping to find a rising political star to marry or to set in motion their own career ambitions, she was in her mid- to late twenties and still had a look of innocence about her. She smiled hesitantly, proving once and for all that her tough talk on the phone had been an act designed to put off an unpleasant chore, not real hostility.

Dressed in jeans, a bright orange T-shirt, and running shoes and wearing almost no visible makeup on her flawless complexion, she didn't look at all like a woman who cared about clothes or cosmetics. She probably didn't even need hairspray for that careless short style she wore that emphasized lovely green eyes. Amanda wondered again about those two overburdened suitcases.

Apparently Ms. Baldwin caught her astonishment. "I know," she said with the faintest trace of an unidentifiable accent. "Isn't that just awful? I can never make up my mind what to take on a trip like this. I mean, we're going to the beach, for heaven's sake. I'll probably live in a bathing suit and shorts, but I have dressy slacks, at least a dozen blouses, one good dress, and enough shoes to stock the window at Pay-Less." She glanced at Amanda's carry-on bag with envy. "I'll never be able to travel like that."

"You'll learn," Amanda said, glad to be on a topic that

would put her source at ease. "Especially after the airlines lose your bags a few times."

"I suppose."

"We don't have a lot of time. Could we talk a little about what you do for Senator Rawlings?"

"Actually, I work for Ms. LaPalma. I type and file, that sort of thing. Occasionally she has me do a little research for her. I've only been here a few months, just since I finished grad school in political science."

"Then you don't have much contact with the senator?"

"Well, sure, I see him almost every day. He likes to wander through the office, say hello. He figures it builds morale, shows he's just one of the troops. I think he just gets tired of sitting in that lonely ol' office of his and listening to all those windbags."

"The other senators?"

"Them, plus the lobbyists and that Mr. Fine." She blushed furiously. "Sorry. I don't suppose I should have said that. Can we keep it off the record?"

Amanda grinned. "That's okay. I'm not here to report every slip of the tongue."

"What are you looking to write about?"

"Mary Allison. How well did you know her?"

"Personally, not all that well. But her clerk, that's Jonathan Lindsey, he's the one who's coming to pick me up. He's my best friend. Not really a boyfriend or anything. I mean, we're not serious. Anyway, he's told me lots and lots about her. He thought she was just about the best thing to come out of Georgia since peaches. Had a big ol' crush on her, if you ask me, but he wouldn't ever admit it, seeing as how she was engaged and everything.''

Amanda wondered if he could have been distraught enough over the impending marriage to have killed her in a jealous rage. It was yet another angle to consider, even if it didn't appeal to her nearly as much as thinking of Greg Fine nudging Mary Allison's car into that tree. She hoped he'd turn up soon so she could get a firsthand look at him and a chance to ask a question or two.

''Tell me something,'' she said to the suddenly talkative Leslie Baldwin. ''Were you ever alone with Senator Rawlings?''

The young woman's green eyes widened. ''You mean like on a date or something?''

Even Amanda had to laugh at that image. ''No, not a date. I meant did you ever have to take reports into his office, maybe drop off a file?''

''Why, sure. Usually I'd just leave it with Ms. Wilcox, but sometimes she'd tell me to take it right on in because it was something he was anxious for.''

Amanda searched for a careful way to proceed. ''Was he polite?''

''Why, sure he was.''

''Did any of your colleagues ever complain that he wasn't so polite to them?''

''Never.''

''Did he ever comment on personal things, for instance, the way you were dressed?'' she asked, picking the most innocuous symptom of harassment as a place to begin.

"I suppose he might have told me I looked real pretty once or twice. Why?"

She looked genuinely puzzled. Either she was oblivious to what constituted sexual harassment or she'd never heard so much as a hint that the senator was guilty of it. It was apparent to Amanda, anyway, that Leslie Baldwin hadn't been a victim.

"It doesn't matter," she told her now. "I appreciate your time. I'll get back to you if I have any more questions."

"Don't you want to stay and meet Jonathan? His car just pulled up." She was already gathering up her luggage.

"Sure," Amanda said, and followed her to the door.

The young man who brushed an impersonal kiss across Leslie Baldwin's cheek barely glanced at Amanda, until Leslie introduced her. Then his gaze narrowed.

"Why would you want to smear the name of a wonderful woman like Mary Allison?" he demanded.

"That's not my intention at all," Amanda promised him. "But I think there's reason to believe her death was neither a suicide nor an accident. I want to get to the bottom of it."

His jaw went slack at that. The blood seemed to drain out of his face. "She wasn't . . . she didn't kill herself?"

"I'm still looking for all the proof I need, but I don't think so," Amanda said gently.

"Omigosh," Leslie murmured, her gaze never leaving her friend's ashen face. "Jonathan, you were right."

Amanda kept her eyes pinned on the young man, who

had reportedly adored his boss. He looked absolutely stricken. "You thought she had been murdered?" she asked him.

He shook his head. "Not exactly. I just knew she would never have killed herself. Then when all those reports came in saying that she had, I told myself I must not have known her as well as I thought I did."

"Is there anyone you can think of who might have wanted her dead? Anyone at all?"

"Everybody who worked with her adored her. She was smart and kind and generous."

All the words of a man with a terrible crush, Amanda thought, not paying them much heed. "Surely she had some enemies. That's the nature of politics, isn't it?"

"People in Washington don't go out and kill someone just for having opposing ideas," he retorted. "If they did, we'd have to elect a new Congress every session."

"Maybe she stepped on somebody's toes. She was ambitious, right?"

"Sure, but everybody here is. Again, nobody would kill just to get ahead."

"What if she knew something that would threaten someone's career?"

"Like what?"

"She's heard the sexual harassment rumor," Leslie Baldwin said. "She even asked me if the senator had come on to me." She glanced at Amanda. "Not that you ever used those words."

Amanda accepted the rebuke. She deserved it. "I didn't

want to put words into your mouth," she explained. She vowed to herself never again to leap to conclusions about a single soul. Sweet Ms. Baldwin had surprised her with her astuteness.

She caught the look of amusement that passed between the two clerks. "Okay, what else did I miss?"

"You wouldn't have had any way of knowing," Leslie said, already providing her with an excuse, even though Amanda still didn't know exactly what blunder she'd committed.

"Come on," she told them. "Spill it."

Jonathan was the one who got to rub it in. "Senator Rawlings is Leslie's grandfather."

Amanda groaned. "No wonder you didn't take exception to his comments on the way you looked."

"I'm sorry not to tell you right off," she apologized, "but it's not something we like to spread around. I don't want anyone thinking I get special favors. Grandfather's as tough on me as he is on anyone in that office."

"But the others do know?"

"Most of them, yes."

"So you'd be the last person they'd complain to," Amanda said.

Leslie shook her head vehemently. "Not at all. Oh, at first everyone walked on eggshells around me, but then they heard me gripe about this and that, and pretty soon they forgot all about who I was."

"But no one would tell you if they felt your grandfather was harassing them, would they?"

"Not because we're related," she retorted, angry color rising in her cheeks. "Because it never happened."

Jonathan was nodding as well. "I've been there longer than Leslie. The only person I've ever heard even hint at it was Ms. LaPalma, but she never said it happened to her. It was always just some vague remark that was impossible to substantiate."

"Then you don't think Mary Allison was harassed? Or that she intended to make her allegations public?"

"Absolutely not," Jonathan said. "Whoever told you that was lying."

Either the whole damned office had joined in the conspiracy to protect the senator or Valerie LaPalma had made up not only the allegations themselves, but the threat of those allegations being made public.

But why? What did Valerie LaPalma have to gain by stirring up this particular hornet's nest?

CHAPTER

Twelve

FOR the first twenty minutes of her flight to Atlanta, Amanda tried to figure out exactly how Valerie LaPalma fit into the story. Had she deliberately lied to send Amanda off on a wild goose chase? But, according to Jonathan, she'd floated those harassment charges long before Amanda had come on the scene. What, then, was her real agenda? An image of her leaving Mrs. Watkins's house after the funeral with Zachary Downs suddenly came to mind. Were the two of them in on some scheme to discredit Senator Rawlings and assure Zack's ascendance to the Senate Foreign Affairs Committee?

Interestingly, that was exactly what Valerie had accused Mary Allison of doing, Amanda recalled. Had she hoped that simply by spreading the rumor, she could get Mary Allison fired? When that hadn't worked, had she taken action to see that she was permanently removed?

All fascinating questions, Amanda decided. Maybe the

answers would come when she discovered more about the car that had bumped Mary Allison's off that Georgia back road. It occurred to her that no one yet had even hinted why Mary Allison would have been on that particular road. Dee-Ann Watkins thought her daughter had simply gone for a drive to clear her head.

Since it seemed clear to Amanda that Mary Allison hadn't gone to that deserted road to commit suicide, was it possible she had been lured there on some pretext or another? She'd have to question Dee-Ann Watkins in more detail about that afternoon, though surely she would have told the police at once of anything suspicious. But perhaps Mary Allison had mentioned some seemingly insignificant errand to her mother or even to Lou-Ellen Kinsale, something they both might have forgotten about in the chaotic aftermath of her death.

In the meantime, Amanda had to get the search for the rental car under way. She picked up the in-flight telephone and called *Inside Atlanta*.

"Well, it's about time you called back," Jenny Lee informed her indignantly. "I've been sitting around here twiddling my thumbs ever since I gave you that information on Gregory Fine."

"Why?"

"Why? Because I work for you, that's why. Or had you forgotten that I'm *your* research assistant? I've been waiting for you to let me know what you wanted me to do next. Another hour and Oscar was going to fire the temp and put me back on that ol' switchboard."

Amanda hadn't considered that possibility when she'd hung up after talking with Jenny Lee the day before. She was still adjusting to the whole idea of having an assistant, especially one so ambitious and anxious to please. Jenny Lee considered Amanda her mentor and clearly felt hurt that she'd been left out of the planning on this story.

"I'm sorry," Amanda apologized. "Believe me, though, I am about to make up for it. I hope you didn't have plans for the Labor Day weekend."

"Nothing that can't be changed," Jenny Lee said immediately, an edge of excitement already returning to her voice. "What's going on?"

"We need to find a silver car, probably a rental, with a dent in it. Most likely the damage would be to the right front fender, maybe the whole right side."

"You have any haystacks you want me to search for an itty-bitty needle?"

Amanda refused to be daunted. All it would take would be persistence and a little luck. "I'm guessing the car would have been rented a week ago today, maybe even last Saturday morning. I'll check with the airport rental agencies when I land and try to find out where they send cars for repairs. In the meantime, you start working body shops, especially any with a reputation for quick repairs and discretion. If you get any leads, you might want to check 'em out in person, do a little snooping around before you start asking questions."

"Got it. Anything else?"

"If you find a suspicious car, get Larry to shoot some

pictures, and be sure to get the tag number, any rental ID, that sort of thing,'' she advised, knowing Jenny Lee would be thrilled to have a chance to spend some on-the-job time with her favorite free-lance photographer. That alone would make up for any ruined holiday plans.

''What exactly are we working on?'' Jenny Lee asked.

Amanda was amused by the fact that her assistant had left that question for last. She was obviously far more interested in the chase than the goal. Jenny Lee had discovered an adventurous streak in herself within days of teaming up with Amanda. Amanda prayed she wouldn't live to regret it.

''I just heard from Jim Harrison. It's beginning to look as if Mary Allison Watkins was nudged off that road, either by a hit-and-run driver or by someone who wanted her dead. I'm betting on the latter.''

''You mean this might be the proof we need that she was actually murdered?'' Jenny Lee said in a hushed tone.

''Could be. We'll know more when we find that car and figure out who was driving it.''

''Oh, my gosh, does Oscar know?''

''Not yet. Put him on so I can fill him in.''

''Amanda, where the hell are you?'' Oscar demanded as if she'd been avoiding him purposely. ''I've been calling that hotel for hours now. I even had security check the damn room. By the way, they told me it hadn't been slept in one night. I don't mind telling you, I almost had a heart attack when they told me that. How would I explain to Donelli that you'd been kidnapped?''

"You knew perfectly well that I hadn't been," she reminded him. "You'd just talked to me yesterday."

He ignored the interruption. Apparently he was on a roll and wasn't going to be satisfied until he'd finished his lecture.

"The only thing that kept me from calling the police was the fact that some fancy doorman told security he'd seen you leaving with a Frenchman in a limo the size of Rhode Island." His voice practically shook with indignation. "Would you care to explain what you were doing out overnight with that arms dealer, when you've just been married a couple of months?"

Though she knew she ought to be grateful, Amanda cursed the efficiency of the hotel security staff. "I told you that Armand arranged for me to interview Valerie LaPalma," she explained patiently. "As for the rest, I'm not sure that's something I need to explain to you, especially since my husband knows all about it." Well, not exactly everything, but close enough. "Anyway, I was not with Armand all night. I was on his plane flying to France. Alone, unless you want to count Henri."

"Who the hell is Henri?"

It was interesting to see which of the facts she'd just doled out registered first. Oscar's loyalty to Donelli was one of his best qualities. She could hardly wait until he realized she'd mentioned flying to France. He'd been so caught up in the details of the charges against Blaine Rawlings the day before, he'd apparently missed where she'd been when she'd discovered them.

"Henri is one of Armand's employees. You remember, the guy he sent down to watch out for me a few months ago."

"Oh, yeah. So you went to France with this Henri?"

"Right," she said calmly.

Dead silence greeted the confirmation. Then, "Did you say *France?* As in Paris? As in Europe?" he inquired in a voice filled with disbelief.

"That's the place. Maybe you're the one we should have teaching Pete about geography."

"Explain," he said.

"It's too long a story to get into now. I'll tell you when I get back."

"And just when will that be?"

"I'm on a plane, heading home right now."

"You're calling from a damned airplane? Do you know how much that costs? First a trip to goddamned France, and now you're chatting away from thirty thousand feet. I don't believe this. Have you lost all sense of reality? You don't work for the blasted *New York Times*. We don't have unlimited resources around here."

"What I'm spending will be peanuts compared to the amount of money we make with increased circulation when this story breaks." To prove it, she summarized what she knew so far. The tension crackling over the line seemed to lessen.

"I think we're going to nail a big one this time," she concluded, just in case he'd missed the point.

"Well, I've got a little news for you that might play

right into your hands," he said, immediately forgetting all about his prior objections and getting into the spirit of the hunt. "We just got word that Senator Rawlings is planning a press conference today for five o'clock out at his Atlanta estate. Actually, they called it a photo opportunity, but it amounts to the same thing."

"He's probably just announcing some pork barrel deal he got for the home state."

"Could be, but that's not the rumor that's circulating. Word has it he's going to announce his intention to retire at the end of this term. Instead of kicking off his campaign today, he's going to end it."

Amanda figured it cost them at least twenty dollars in long-distance charges just for the amount of time she sat there with her mouth hanging open. "You're kidding, right?"

"It's not that big a surprise," Oscar cautioned. "The man's sixty-eight. Maybe he figures he's due for some time to sit down by the river and smell those prize roses of his."

"It's the timing. Doesn't it suggest to you that he's on the run from the sexual harassment allegations that could surface at any moment, to say nothing of the possibility of being involved in a murder conspiracy? Maybe he figures if he creeps out of the limelight, the whole furor will go away. He doesn't stand a chance of that if he keeps on campaigning. Who slipped you the word on this?"

"A reliable source in Washington, according to my reliable source in Atlanta."

Amanda considered that about two steps removed from any kind of proof. Nagging little doubts began to surface. "Oscar, maybe we shouldn't get too excited about this. Maybe it really is just a photo op."

"You want to pass?" he asked slyly.

"Of course not," she admitted.

"I didn't think so. What time are you landing?"

She glanced at her watch. "Four oh-five, if we're on time. We took off a few minutes late, though, and if this turbulence is anything to judge by, we're probably going to wind up coming back by way of Tennessee."

"Assuming you fly in a straighter line than that, I'll send Larry out that way to pick you up and take you out to the senator's. Maybe you can wrangle a few minutes alone with him after the press conference. You sure don't want to bring up your suspicions in front of all those other reporters."

"Damn right," she said. "I'll call you as soon as I have anything. If it looks like we're not going to make up that delay in Washington or if we're going to get diverted by the weather, I'll call back and maybe you can get Jenny Lee over there to keep an eye on what happens."

Amanda made the suggestion for backup because it was the prudent thing to do, but she had every intention of being at Blaine Rawlings's home at five o'clock if she had to fly the damned plane home herself.

Fortunately for everyone on board, the pilot touched down at four-twenty. Amanda broke for the exit the instant the seat belt light went out. She was out of the terminal in record time. She spotted Larry arguing with a policeman about his chosen parking space right in front of the main entrance. Apparently the cop did not consider a media identification card a license to linger in a no-parking zone.

Amanda cut the discussion short by joining them and tossing her bags into the car. "Thanks for your help," she told the still blustering officer, who had his ticket book out and his pen in hand. They pulled away before he could carry out his threat. It was just as well. Larry never paid the damned things anyway, if the neat little pile on the dashboard was any indication.

On the drive to Senator Rawlings's estate, Amanda filled Larry in on the investigation.

"But Oscar thinks this guy's gonna announce his retirement this afternoon," the photographer said, clearly confused. "Why would he do that if he knows you won't be able to substantiate the allegations against him?"

"Maybe he thinks I'll print them anyway. It's way too late to try to fight that kind of scandal. He'd probably rather walk away," she said.

But for the second time since she'd heard the rumor, she realized something about it didn't ring true. The Blaine Rawlings she'd encountered was a scrapper. He liked nothing better than a good brawl, especially if he felt he was on the side of truth, justice, and the American way. He wouldn't walk away meekly before the fight even got started.

Well, she would know soon enough, she decided as they

reached the lavish country home with its sweeping lawns, lovingly tended rose gardens, and comfortable chairs down on the riverbank. Judging from the number of cars lining the country road leading up to the house, the media had turned out in force for the senator's announcement.

It wasn't until she was crossing the lawn toward all the noise in back that Amanda began to get an inkling that somebody had gotten today's schedule of events all wrong, quite possibly deliberately.

The phrase *photo opportunity* came to mind again, along with Oscar's cynical suggestion that it had been a cover for something much more. A school bus parked in front of the house suggested otherwise, as did the outbursts of childish glee that filled the air.

She exchanged a glance with Larry. "Those are not the sounds of a man delivering a eulogy for his own senatorial career."

C H A P T E R

Thirteen

AS Amanda and Larry rounded the corner of Senator Rawlings's stately old house, they ran smack into his housekeeper, who looked exhausted but as if she were having the time of her life.

"Hello, Velma," Amanda said.

The old black woman gave her a once-over. "You're that reporter who was here once before," she said, referring to the time Amanda had come to question the senator about an illegal arms deal. "Amanda Roberts, isn't it? From that magazine?"

"Yes, ma'am. What's going on?"

"The senator's hosting a picnic for the children from several of the shelters around town. Does it every year. He usually don't like reporters here, but that publicity chief of his, Martin Oates, he insisted this year, what with the campaign getting into full swing. You go on out. I'm sure Mr. Oates will be glad to see you."

Amanda noticed that Velma didn't seem to think the senator would be nearly as delighted. Perhaps she remembered Amanda's unceremonious departure the last time, when the senator had called the FBI to haul her away.

Larry glanced at Amanda when Velma was gone, then gestured toward the dozens of children smeared with ice cream and drenched from unplanned dips in the river. Harried adults drifted among them, though their expressions indicated they knew they had long since lost all control.

"Looks like a photo op all right," he said. "You want to split? TV will have it tonight. The papers will have it tomorrow."

"True, but you might get the kinds of shots that could be pretty poignant down the road, if the senator is brought down by scandal."

Larry grinned. "That's what I love about you. You're sentimental to the core."

For some reason, the comment grated. It made Amanda feel more like a media vulture than usual. "Just go take your pictures."

"And where will you be?"

"Drinking lemonade and soaking up atmosphere," she retorted, and wandered off in search of Martin Oates or Gregory Fine. Perhaps they could explain the rumors about Senator Rawlings's supposedly imminent retirement.

She hadn't gone far when she caught sight of Rawlings himself, back in his khaki pants and red suspenders, his shirt-sleeves rolled up. He was leading a parade of little girls, all dressed in their Sunday best, through his elaborate rose gardens, pointing out each bush by name and encouraging them to pick whatever one they wanted.

"Careful of those thorns, though," he warned as they scattered among the bushes. He watched them go, a spark of amusement in his tired eyes. Eventually he turned his gaze on Amanda, and she wondered if he'd known she was there all along.

"Can't start 'em too young learning to appreciate nature's beauty," he told her.

"Do you think these girls will grow up to have time to stop and smell the roses?" she asked.

"I surely do hope so," he said, then sighed heavily. "The world's a troubled place, when folks can abuse little ones like these. A picnic like this isn't much in the overall scheme of things, but who knows, maybe it'll make a difference to one or two of them. Sometimes happy memories are all we have to keep us going, no matter how well off we are financially. Come along. Take a walk with me down by the river. Maybe there's a breeze stirring down there."

Surprised but pleased by the friendly invitation, Amanda fell into step beside him. "How long have you been doing this?"

"Ten years. Started it the year before my wife died. It was her idea. She said legislation and money were one thing, but it was time and caring that were really important to little ones. She used to volunteer two and three days a week at these same shelters. Said it like to broke her heart, but she went back time after time. She was a strong woman, much stronger than I am.''

Amanda wondered about that. She was beginning to think that Senator Blaine Rawlings had an inner core, based on rock-solid southern values, that she had greatly underestimated. She was also beginning to doubt that such a man would ever resort to sexual harassment on the job, much less be involved in a conspiracy to commit murder. As much as it annoyed her to have to admit it, he did seem to epitomize the old-fashioned southern gentleman.

''I met your granddaughter earlier today,'' she told him.

His nostalgic expression brightened immediately. ''You met Leslie? By God, she's a smart one, isn't she? Takes after her old grandfather, if I do say so myself. One of these days I expect she'll be entering politics, though not from Georgia. Her fool mama went and married a damn Yankee. Leslie was born and raised in New Hampshire, of all places. It astonishes me she hasn't turned out to be a Republican. Guess I got to her early enough,'' he said with a chuckle. ''First stuffed toy I gave her was a donkey.''

His laughter died, and he regarded Amanda thoughtfully. ''You interviewing her about Mary Allison?''

''Yes.''

''What'd she tell you?''

''Not much. She talked more about her boss, Valerie LaPalma, and about Jonathan. He came by to pick her up while I was there.'' She dropped both names, hoping to gauge the senator's reaction. Unfortunately, not one eyelash flickered. Not one muscle in his cheek twitched. As a trial balloon, her attempt had failed miserably. She decided to try again, this time with a more direct approach.

"Tell me something: How would you compare Mary Allison and Valerie?"

His brow knit. "Compare how?"

"Work habits, personality, whatever."

"Both of them are . . . were, I guess you'd say in Mary Allison's case . . . smart as the dickens. Mary Allison was the quieter of the two. Valerie's all flash and dazzle. I'd say she's the more ambitious one, but Mary Allison was the one I expected to have a real future. She kept at things, nice and methodical, never missed a detail. Valerie can find the substance in an issue, but she doesn't have the patience to sell it the way Mary Allison did. If there's a shortcut, Valerie'd be the one to find it."

Amanda thought she heard real affection in Blaine Rawlings's voice when he spoke of Mary Allison, along with genuine respect. She wasn't entirely sure she heard either when he was assessing Valerie.

"Were they rivals?" she asked.

"Maybe on Valerie's part. Mary Allison never met a person she didn't like. She believed in her own strengths. She didn't need a lot of outside approval."

His analysis was directly contradictory to the way Valerie had described her own and Mary Allison's personalities. His seemed to jibe more with what Amanda had been hearing from others. Once again she wondered just what Valerie LaPalma was up to and whether some rivalry between the two women had turned deadly.

"What about Greg Fine? Did he feel threatened by either of them?" she asked.

The senator's gaze narrowed. "What are you getting at?"

"He's a pretty intense, competitive man. I was just wondering how he got along with two ambitious, assertive women."

"Greg knows his place on my staff is secure," Rawlings said curtly.

The terse remark reminded Amanda of what she'd heard about how Fine had gotten the job in the first place. "He's been with you a long time?"

"Must be pretty close to fifteen years now."

"I understand he was with one of those big Wall Street law firms before he joined your staff."

"He was, and he was fired over some nonsense about insider trading." He leveled a gaze straight at her. "I'll guarantee you Greg never leaked anything, but somebody in that law firm did and let Greg take the fall."

His spin on the story and the fact that he'd guessed what she was after left Amanda openmouthed. "You're sure of that?"

"I would not have hired him if I hadn't been," he said so vehemently that Amanda was forced to reconsider her assessment not only of the senator, but of Greg Fine. At this rate she was going to end up liking both men. The possibility chilled her. There wasn't a politician on the face of the earth she wanted to like or trust.

"You satisfied?" the senator inquired, regarding her with some amusement.

"For the moment."

"Good. Now go get you some of Velma's fried chicken and peach cobbler. They're the best in the state of Georgia, maybe even the whole darned South."

Amanda was afraid of that. If they were that good, some journalistic purists would say they constituted a bribe. Still, she eyed the buffet tables longingly. She hadn't had a bite to eat since morning. Mouthwatering temptation lured her across the lawn. She was so intent on the chicken that she missed the diminutive white-haired woman determinedly coming her way.

"Amanda!"

Only one woman in the universe could drawl her name with quite such an imperious note: Miss Martha Wellington. Amanda had grown genuinely fond of the local historian and society grande dame, but when Miss Martha got that tone in her voice, inevitably Amanda was in for a lecture on some sin or another.

Stopped in her tracks, Amanda waited for Miss Martha to catch up. She moved pretty quickly for a woman in her eighties, even though she needed a cane to steady herself—or so she claimed. At the moment, she was waving it at Amanda.

"I am surprised at you," she declared, planting the cane into the ground with such force that Amanda was glad she'd stepped out of the way.

"What have I done now?"

"I understand you're raising some kind of ruckus about that poor girl's death."

"If you're talking about Mary Allison, I am investigating why she died," she said, keeping her voice astonishingly even. Miss Martha tended to think she got to decide which stories Amanda pursued. Obviously this wasn't one she would have chosen.

"Why?" Miss Martha demanded. "What's to be gained?"

"The truth."

"What truth?"

"There's only one."

"You know that's not so, girl. What if all your snooping tarnishes the reputation of one of the finest politicians this state has ever had?"

"How could it do that, unless he's done something wrong?"

Miss Martha shot her a look of disgust. "Oh, fiddle-faddle. You know all it takes is a whiff of scandal to destroy years of hard work. Doesn't matter a hang if it's true or not."

"Miss Martha, I am not out to destroy Senator Rawlings. In fact, much to my amazement, I'm actually starting to like the man."

"Then drop all this foolishness and let the dead rest in peace."

"Did he ask you to talk to me?"

Miss Martha drew herself up indignantly. "Nobody tells me what to do, young lady. I'm talking to you because I don't want to see you make a fool of yourself and take a decent man along with you."

"It sounds as if you have some idea what I might report. How would you know that unless there's some truth to it?"

"Oh, for goodness' sakes, do you think I've lived this many years without getting to know a lot of people?" she retorted impatiently. "I've had half a dozen calls this morning alone."

Terrific, Amanda thought. At this rate every newsperson in the state, if not the country, would have all the details of this story in print or on the air before she did.

Miss Martha waved a bejeweled finger in her face. "I know what you're thinking. You're worried about getting beat by the competition, as if that's what's important. Do you suppose it matters who writes the story first, if the whole thing is a pack of lies?"

"But whose lies?" Amanda asked. "That's what I'm trying to figure out."

Miss Martha sighed heavily. "You're not going to give this up, are you?"

"No, ma'am, I'm not. I'm sorry."

"I never thought I'd say this, but I am bitterly disappointed in you, Amanda,'' she said with a quiver of emotion in her voice.

That was nothing to what Amanda felt when Miss Martha turned her back on her and stalked away, her back as straight and regal as a queen's.

CHAPTER

Fourteen

*J*ENNY Lee was a very ingenious liar. It was a dubious talent in most people, but it was one Amanda could admire. The secret of a good prevarication, especially for journalistic purposes, was to stick as close to the truth as possible. Amanda walked into the *Inside Atlanta* newsroom an hour after leaving Blaine Rawlings's party to find her assistant on the phone, fibbing up a storm and obviously having the time of her life doing it.

"What's your name again, hon? . . . Johnny. Well, Johnny, I'm calling from *Inside Atlanta,* you know, the magazine. Well, one of our people rented a car this past weekend and put a little dent in it, and I'm trying like the dickens to track it down and make sure it's taken care of."

Amanda couldn't hear the other end of the conversation, but she could imagine it. Jenny Lee's seductive drawl could coax a saint into unheard-of sins. Poor Johnny, unless he had the hormones of a neutered tomcat, didn't stand a chance.

"Yeah, I know it would be a lot easier if I had the paperwork right here in front of me, but the reporter took off on another assignment and he can't be reached. Communications in some of those war zones aren't all that great, you know what I mean?"

She allowed the images of bombs dropping and artillery shellings to linger for just a moment. Amanda had to admit it was a nice touch. She couldn't have done any better.

"Anyway, hon, my boss is a real stickler for not letting something like this go," Jenny Lee continued. "If you could check around and see what you've got there, I'd really appreciate it. You must keep some kind of accident records on your rentals, right? The insurance companies all require so much paperwork these days, don't they? Anyway, all I know for sure is that the car was silver. . . . Sure, I'll wait, hon."

She glanced up at Amanda and held her hand over the receiver. "Since you had to get to that press conference, I thought you probably wouldn't have time to do the rental agencies, so I just started on them."

"Did you strike out with the body shops?"

Jenny Lee looked hurt that Amanda had doubted her ability to get any information she set out to get. "Have you ever known me to give up?" she demanded indignantly. "I've got a source over at the police department who's digging around for the names of the shops the police routinely check in cases like this. I figured I might's well start with those, instead of wasting time guessing from their ads in the phone book. He should be calling back any minute now.''

She held up her hand to silence Amanda's reply. "I'm here, Johnny. . . . No record of an accident last weekend. Any of your cars out longer than you'd expected? . . . I see. Any drop-offs you were expecting back here, but got turned in in another city? . . . Okay, hon. Thanks for your trouble. Lord knows where he got that car. I'm going to wring his neck for not using you the way he was supposed to.''

"I'm impressed," Amanda told her when she'd hung up. "I'd never have thought of that bit about a drop-off.''

Jenny Lee shrugged. "Seems to me like a smart thing to do. It might cost a little more, but at least there wouldn't be a record at the Atlanta rental agency of any repairs needed. If they had the repairs done themselves, someone here might even notice that, whereas another agency wouldn't know when they'd been made.''

Jenny Lee's logic was on the money. "How many agencies have you called?" Amanda asked.

"I'm halfway through the list in the Yellow Pages. I'm only doing the majors. I think the person we're looking for would use a place with high volume. Less risk of being noticed. Besides, some of those other operations really stick it to people over every little scratch. That'd be too risky in this case.''

Amanda nodded. "Good thinking.''

"One thing occurred to me, though," Jenny Lee said

worriedly. "It's not like the drive from D.C. to Atlanta takes days. What if somebody drove their own car down here?"

"I don't even want to think about that," Amanda said. "But you're right, it is a possibility. If we strike out on the rentals, I'll start looking around in Washington to see what kind of cars our suspects own."

Just then Oscar slammed down his phone and headed across the newsroom. "What happened at the press conference?"

"The senator played host to dozens of hyperactive little children from area child abuse shelters." Amanda grinned. "The word *retirement* did not cross his lips. In fact, this looked very much like a campaign kick-off to me."

"What the hell happened?"

"I'd say you ought to develop new sources. It was not entirely in vain, though. I did get to have a nice little chat with Rawlings."

She described her conversation with the politician and the subsequent one with Miss Martha, whom Oscar knew all too well. She was one of the few people in the world who could terrorize him with her imperious demands.

"I'm seriously beginning to wonder about those harassment charges," she concluded. "Maybe they were trumped up. Maybe Mary Allison never intended to say anything."

"I don't get it," Oscar said, looking puzzled.

"Believe me, the scenarios don't make a lot of sense to me yet, either, but one thing's for sure, Mary Allison is dead.'' Using Oscar as a sounding board, she tried out various possibilities. ''Either somebody feared she was about to expose the senator or somebody made up those charges hoping they'd get her killed or that they'd force the senator into retirement.''

''Who'd benefit from his retirement?''

''His political opponents. Maybe Zach Downs.''

''How do you figure that?''

''The opponents are obvious, but the way I hear it, Downs is running for the Senate this time in Alabama. He expects to win. When he gets there, he wants to be a power broker in foreign affairs. That would take longer if Blaine Rawlings was still in his way.''

''That's an ugly scenario, especially since Mary Allison was engaged to Downs.''

''I know,'' Amanda conceded. ''But I don't think we can ignore the possibility.''

Just as she and Oscar concluded their conversation, Jenny Lee got off the phone. Triumphantly she waved a piece of paper. ''I've got those body shops. There are six of 'em. Larry's finishing up in the lab at home. He says he'll be here in a half hour with your prints from the party. He'll go with me to check out the body shops.'' She looked at Amanda. ''You want to come with us?''

Amanda could tell Jenny Lee was just itching to go off on her own to investigate. Fortunately Amanda had another angle or two she wanted to pursue.

''Nope,'' she said. ''You and Larry can handle that. I think I'm going out for a cup of coffee.''

Oscar and Jenny Lee regarded her incredulously. "Why?" they said in unison. Coffee breaks were not something she indulged in midway through an investigation. She usually just grabbed a handful of her favorite gourmet jelly beans and kept right on going.

"Because I just remembered something Pete said the other night before I left town. He used to see the senator in the coffee shop down the street from his office all the time, usually with Mary Allison or Valerie LaPalma. I'd like an independent view of how the senator treated his staffers. Waitresses tend to have a pretty good memory about their regulars, especially if they happen to be famous."

Jenny Lee nodded. "Why don't Larry and I meet up with you later out at your place? We'll bring the pizza. Oscar, you want to come, too?"

He looked tempted, especially by the pizza, but he shook his head. "My wife's back in town. She's planning to drag me to the country club tonight. If I don't show up, I'll never hear the end of it."

Amanda patted his hand consolingly. "Living the good life certainly is a trial, isn't it?" she said, referring to his wife's moneyed background and her refusal to extricate herself from an exclusionary social scene that harked back to another era in the South.

"Don't be smug, Amanda. At least my wife knows where I am most of the time, which is more than I can say for your husband. Donelli called here not fifteen minutes ago wanting to know where the hell you were."

"Why didn't you tell me? I was sitting right here."

"Because I filled him in myself," he said smugly. "I left out that part about France."

"How thoughtful!"

"I thought I ought to give you a little more time to work out an explanation that makes sense. I'll be wanting to hear one myself first thing in the morning," he told her as he strolled out the door.

Amanda scowled after him. "One of these days I'm going to get a job where my boss doesn't think my husband walks on water. Better yet, I'm not even going to introduce them."

She made a quick call to the house, hoping to get Pete rather than her husband. She didn't have time to waste on all those explanations right now. Fortunately Pete loved to answer the phone.

"Tell me again about that coffee shop where you used to see Senator Rawlings," she said.

He described the location with astonishing attention to detail. By the time he was done, she practically knew how many cracks there were in the sidewalk between Peachtree Center and the restaurant. He definitely had the makings of a sleuth or a reporter. In Amanda's experience, sometimes that amounted to the same career choice.

"How about I meet you there?" he inquired hopefully.

"Sorry. I don't have time to wait for you. I'll be home soon. Thanks again for the tip."

"I told you before, you need me."

He said it with his usual arrogant tone, but Amanda was

almost certain she heard a wistful note in his voice. How could she make a thirteen-year-old who obviously felt he'd never been important to anyone believe that he mattered to her? Quick reassurances wouldn't do it. Sometimes she wondered if even time would heal all of Pete's wounds or if he'd ever trust Amanda and Joe enough to reveal just how deep those wounds went.

The Peachtree Deli was getting ready to close when Amanda walked in about seven o'clock. There was one customer left at the counter with a cup of coffee and a thick wedge of cheesecake. A middle-aged, red-haired waitress, who looked as if her feet hurt, was wiping off the tables, refilling salt and pepper shakers, and stocking the little sugar holders with packages of the fake stuff. The honest-to-God sugar was in a large glass shaker. Obviously this was a place that knew its customers' habits. The iced tea probably came already sweetened.

The waitress caught sight of Amanda, and her expression turned sour.

"We're closed," she announced firmly.

"That's okay. I'm really just interested in a little information. Maybe you could sit a minute and chat?"

The woman looked torn. She clearly wanted to sit, but she was obviously just as anxious to shut down and be on her way. Amanda glanced over the counter and saw that the coffeepot was still full. "We could have a cup of coffee. I'll buy." When that didn't have the desired effect, she added, "And I'm a very generous tipper."

"I suppose a few more minutes won't make much difference," the woman agreed. "Pick a table and I'll be back with the coffee."

When they were both seated, Amanda glanced at her nametag. "Sally, I'm with *Inside Atlanta*. I'm doing research on a story, and I was hoping somebody here might be able to help. I know it's late and you're anxious to get home, but I really would appreciate your time."

At the mention of the magazine, Sally's expression perked up slightly. "I'll tell you whatever I can. What're you looking for?"

"A friend of mine says he's seen Senator Rawlings eating here once in a while. Do you know him?"

"Sure. He comes in here all the time. Loves the corned beef on rye with an extra pickle."

"Is he usually by himself?"

"Nah. He's always got somebody from his staff with him taking notes like crazy. The man never wastes a minute. Can't even take time to eat in peace. I told him that was a good way to get an ulcer, but he just laughs and says he has a cast-iron stomach. We go through the same conversation every time. It's like a routine or something."

"How does he get along with the people on his staff?"

Sally's weary hazel eyes turned thoughtful. "Well, now, it seems to me like they get along okay, though that chief of staff of his, Mr. Fine . . ." She shook her head. "How anybody could get along with that little twerp is beyond me. Everything has to be prepared just so. Never wants anything the way it comes on the menu, even though it says plain as day, *'No substitutions.'* He asks for un-sweetened iced tea, then turns around and dumps half a container of the stuff in it. The senator used to wink at me every time that Mr. Fine was ordering, like we had a little joke.''

''What about the others?''

''Other than Mr. Fine, most of the time it was that sweet Mary Allison, that poor girl who died last weekend. I couldn't believe it. Like to broke my heart when I read about it. She'd been in here just a couple of days before, by herself that time. Told me she'd come down to make plans for her wedding. Tell the truth, that's what puzzled me about her dying like that. Why would a girl be telling me about her wedding one day and then go and kill herself a couple of days later?''

''It doesn't make sense, does it?'' Amanda agreed. ''Did the senator seem fond of her?''

''Treated her like she was his own daughter. I always had the feeling that was how she felt about him, too, like he was her daddy. Saw in the paper that her own daddy had died a long time ago, so it made sense she'd feel that way about the senator. You should have heard the way the two of them would tease each other sometimes, bickering just like real kin.''

''Bickering, not fighting?''

''Sure, the good-natured kind of squabbles. Mostly, anyway.''

Amanda picked up on the qualification. ''Did they ever have a real fight?''

"As a matter of fact, they did. A couple of weeks ago. Don't quote me on this, because I didn't hear everything they said. I was coming and going like crazy, but it seemed to me like the senator was encouraging her to break off her engagement. Didn't sound like he had a lot of use for that fiancé of hers."

"Is that right?" Amanda said noncommittally. "Anything specific you can remember?"

She shook her head. "No, like I said, I wasn't standing there listening. We were busy that day. One of the girls had called in sick and we couldn't get a replacement in here. I just caught snatches when I'd pass by the table."

Amanda nodded. "You never got the feeling there was anything improper going on between them then?"

Sally looked downright shocked. "Improper? What on earth are you suggesting? The senator's a real gentleman. Believe you me, hon, we get our share of roving hands in this place. I can spot a guy trying to cop a feel quicker than you can say 'More coffee.' The senator wasn't one of 'em. That's not to say I didn't see women making a play for *him* on occasion. Like that Ms. LaPalma." She shook her head, her lips pursed with disapproval. "She used to come in here with him and if all she had on her mind was Senate business, then I'm heir to a fortune. Used to embarrass the dickens out of him."

So, Amanda thought, trying to digest this turn of events. Valerie LaPalma had had the hots for the senator. She had also been the one to plant the idea of the sexual harassment charges in Amanda's head. And she was the same one who had spread the rumors about Mary Allison's intentions throughout the senator's office.

Once again Amanda wondered what Valerie stood to gain by stirring up a scandal, by discrediting both the senator and Mary Allison. Could it have been a simple matter of revenge for unrequited love? It was hard to believe, but stranger things had happened.

Amanda had the feeling that if she could answer both of those questions, she would be well on her way to unraveling the mystery surrounding Mary Allison's death.

C H A P T E R

Fifteen

ALL the way home, Amanda couldn't get Valerie LaPalma out of her mind. Though the delightful prospect of getting back to Donelli intruded frequently, she found herself returning again and again to that picture of Valerie sitting on that terrace in the French countryside, looking perfectly at home in Armand LeConte's world. She also kept recalling her stepping into Zack Downs's limo outside of Dee-Ann Watkins's house the day of Mary Allison's funeral.

Just how friendly were Valerie and Downs? How much did anyone know about the woman, for that matter? A good place to find out more would be Armand LeConte. He couldn't afford to allow anyone into his inner circle without thoroughly checking him out. And yet he trusted Valerie. Amanda suspected that trust was misplaced, but she wondered if she owed it to Armand to tell him so or if that would be the same as tipping the CIA that the leadership in Iraq wasn't pro-American.

She still wasn't sure what to do when she slowly executed the turn into her driveway. Even so, she successfully pushed aside the investigation. Donelli, wearing low-slung jeans and a T-shirt stretched taut across his well-muscled shoulders, was standing on the porch watching as she drove—even more slowly—along the lane to the house. Pete came running out the front door just as she stopped but hung back when Donelli helped her from the car and pulled her into an embrace.

Over Joe's shoulder, Amanda caught sight of the look of longing Pete was trying desperately to hide behind a facade of adolescent disdain. She wanted so badly to reach out to him, but he'd made it clear to both her and Joe that he was more comfortable with rejection than affection. He stuck around because they'd placed no real demands on him. He'd let them both know that he'd vanish at the first sign they were trying to smother him. Amanda thought it was more likely that he was terrified of becoming too attached to them. Whatever had happened in his past, he didn't trust adults not to disappoint him.

"So, guys," she said, linking one arm through Joe's and another through Pete's. She waited, half expecting Pete to shrug off the contact. When he didn't she asked, "What's been happening around here?"

"How much can happen with a bunch of tomatoes and some corn?" Pete replied with disgust as they moved into the comfortable if somewhat shabby living room that

Amanda had vowed to redecorate one of these days when she actually took some time off from work. She'd even bought a stack of the latest decorating magazines to help her with ideas. The last time she'd seen them, they were buried under Joe's farm journals. He'd probably get to them before she did.

Donelli grinned at Pete's reaction. "I'm afraid Pete doesn't quite get the challenge of drought or aphids."

"Hey, man, I'm talking action. Who cares about bugs and stuff?"

"I thought you got plenty of action at that roadside stand," Donelli shot right back. "Last time I passed by, you were pretty busy hustling the tourists."

"Oh?" Amanda said warily, not sure she wanted to hear how the very urban, streetwise teen was adapting to rural farm life. "Hustling how?"

Pete turned his most innocent expression on her. "I was just telling 'em that we have a special process for growing vegetables that makes them healthier than any they could find in town," he explained.

"That doesn't sound like a hustle," Amanda said. "Fresh-picked produce probably *is* healthier. It certainly tastes better."

"Tell her the rest," Donelli told him.

Pete rolled his eyes. "Okay, I was charging them a little more than Joe said I should."

"A little more?" Donelli scoffed. "You could buy gold for what you were charging for that corn."

Amanda tried unsuccessfully to swallow a chuckle. Forget sleuthing, Pete was obviously destined to become a great entrepreneur. "Tell me, were the tourists actually buying this spiel?"

"Buying it?" Donelli said. "He had cars lined up halfway down the highway. He sounded like some traveling medicine man in the old West. You'd have thought our corn cured cancer."

"I made a hundred bucks over what Joe told me to charge, before he made me quit," Pete said proudly. "A guy's gotta think of his future, you know."

Amanda looked from one to the other. "What happened to this windfall?"

Pete's expression lost a little of its smugness. He shot a look of disgust at Donelli. "He made me put it in the bank."

"A savings account is always a smart idea," Amanda said.

"Sure," Pete agreed. "I could have gone for that. But he made me put it in a five-year CD. I'll be old by the time I can get my hands on it."

"You'll be just about ready for college," Joe retorted.

"Right. College is definitely in the cards for me," Pete scoffed. "I ain't even been to junior high."

"Which is painfully obvious, and which we intend to correct in just a few days, isn't that right?" Donelli retorted.

"Like hell," Pete muttered.

"What was that?"

"I said we'll see."

Amanda grinned at them, thinking of the challenge Pete would represent to the school system. "Obviously a lot's gone on while I've been away."

"Forget all that," Pete said, clearly wanting to put that particular discussion on hold. "Did you catch the murderer yet?"

"Not yet. I did follow up on your lead about the coffee shop just now. One of the waitresses there was very helpful."

"All right," Pete said with a whoop. "Told you I could help. Who needs school, when I can work for you and Joe?"

"One lead does not a career make," Donelli reminded him with mock severity. "If you really want to be a private investigator like me, you'll get an education. Then I'll teach you what you need to know to become a PI. You can serve an apprenticeship with me."

"Yeah, sure. When was the last time you took on a case? I'd be better off working for Amanda."

"Then you'll just love journalism school," she replied, deciding this was one battle in which she'd better make it clear she was on Donelli's side. "Four years of college. Maybe graduate school. I tossed in law school, too."

Pete rolled his eyes again. "Okay, okay. Save the lecture. Tell me about this lead of mine. Did it pan out?"

"It certainly raised some interesting questions," she admitted, then told them what the waitress had surmised about Senator Rawlings's relationship with both Mary Allison and Valerie.

"You're planning on digging into this Valerie's life a little more?" Joe guessed.

Amanda nodded. "Something about her bugged me from the first time I saw her after the funeral. And I wasn't real impressed with her when I met her. I still can't figure out what she's doing hiding out in France. Maybe Armand can fill me in." She dropped the mention of France into the middle of the conversation to see if it set off any alarms. It didn't, suggesting that Armand had indeed kept Donelli up to the minute on her whereabouts.

"Do you think LeConte's going to tell you any more than he has already? Obviously she's over there under his protection, and he did give you a shot at her one-on-one to ask your questions."

"But I know more now than I did then, things I'm not even so sure he knows."

Donelli looked skeptical. "My hunch is that he's pretty thorough."

"Then I guess it will depend on what kinds of questions I ask him," Amanda admitted. "He'll shut up tighter than a clam if he thinks I'm trying to pin something on her." She looked at Joe. "Could you play around on that computer of yours and see what you can find before I call him? Just some routine information on her finances might give me some clues about her."

"Sometimes I wonder whether I subscribed to this incredibly expensive data base for you or for my job," he said dryly, referring to his ability to access an amazing amount of computerized record keeping.

"Isn't it nice that it helps us both out," she retorted. "A marriage of convenience, you might say."

"I suppose that's one way of looking at it. Okay, I'll pull up a credit report and whatever else I can find. Naturally you want this yesterday," he said with a sigh of resignation. "And here I'd hoped we'd have a nice family dinner to start the holiday weekend off."

She kissed him. "You weren't going to have that anyway. Jenny Lee and Larry are on their way with pizza and, hopefully, some news about the car that might have been involved in Mary Allison's accident."

Pete's mood cheered considerably at the prospect of sitting around trading clues. Real-life mayhem obviously fascinated him far more than the kinds of games other kids his age spent their evenings playing. It definitely topped his enthusiasm for the educational system. Donelli grinned ruefully at his restored high spirits.

"How about going into the kitchen and checking on our supply of beer and wine?" he suggested.

"There's plenty," Pete retorted immediately.

Amanda regarded him suspiciously. "How would you know that?"

"I was in the refrigerator just a little bit ago getting a soda," he swore, turning on his most innocent expression.

"That better be it," she warned.

"Hey, I'm just a kid."

"You'd do well to remember that occasionally."

Donelli frowned at him. "If the beer and wine are okay, check to make sure all the dishes are done."

"But—"

"Just go."

A grin of sudden understanding broke across Pete's face. "Oh, yeah, I get it. Why didn't you just say you wanted to be alone, man? I can get lost for a while. I know how it is when a guy's been without his babe too long," he said, and headed out the front door, letting the screen door slam behind him.

Laughing, Amanda caught Donelli's face between her hands. "And how is it when a guy's been without his babe too long?"

"It's not something I can explain," he said, pulling her closer. "I'll have to demonstrate."

The demonstration, fascinating and spine-tingling though it was, was cut short by the untimely arrival of Jenny Lee and Larry.

"Whoops," Jenny Lee said, catching sight of Amanda and Joe's flushed faces. "Don't mind us. We'll just go right on into the kitchen and eat this pizza."

"Not without us," Amanda retorted. "I'm starved."

"Yeah," Joe said, casting a rueful glance at her. "So am I. Somehow, though, I don't think pizza's gonna do the trick."

"Later," she promised. "Later."

"So," Amanda asked Jenny Lee and Larry when they were all stuffed with pizza and salad, "how many of the body shops did you get to check out?"

She'd managed to keep silent through the meal only

because Donelli had vowed to strangle her if she brought up business before they were all through eating. Besides, she figured Jenny Lee would have blurted it out if she'd actually found any real news. She'd been willing to wait for any disappointing results of their scouting trip.

Jenny Lee scowled. "We went by all six. Two were closed. There wasn't a sign of a silver car behind the fences, though. We couldn't look inside, because both of them had big, nasty ol' dogs guarding the property."

"And the four that were open?"

"We talked to the owners. All of them swore they hadn't seen a silver car all week."

"They could have been lying," Amanda said.

"Don't you think I know that?" Jenny Lee retorted. "That's why Larry wandered around to check things out, while I kept them talking."

"Not a silver car in sight," he chimed in.

"Do you suppose they could have finished the repairs and returned it already?" Amanda wondered aloud.

"If somebody paid them enough money, they could have rebuilt the whole damned car," Donelli replied. "They've had almost a week to do the work."

Amanda sighed. "What was your gut instinct, Jenny Lee? Were these guys lying to you? Had they worked on a silver car earlier and managed to get it off the lot?"

"These guys were all like your worst nightmare about good ol' boy mechanics. I wouldn't trust 'em to give me their real names, except they all had 'em painted in great big letters on the front of the buildings. Jim Bob's Bodyworks. Joe Don's Fix-It Shop. Sonny's Auto Repairs. Tommy John's Good-as-New Repairs. They didn't waste a lot of time trying to be creative with the company names.'' She shook her head. ''You bet they could have been lying, but I doubt they were going to let me snoop through their paperwork to prove it.''

''Assuming any of 'em kept paperwork on a deal like this,'' Donelli said.

''We have to find that car,'' Amanda said with a moan of dismay. ''It's the only concrete piece of evidence we're likely to find linking somebody to Mary Allison's death. I can come up with motives up the kazoo, but without that link the police aren't going to start hauling people in for questioning.''

''What about checking on the travel records of the key suspects?'' Jenny Lee suggested.

Amanda nodded slowly. ''Maybe. The waitress I talked to tonight said when she saw Mary Allison last week, she was alone. There's a good chance the senator and the rest of his staff were in the Washington office. In fact, the receptionist in the senator's office told me that Gregory Fine was there last Friday. He'd be wherever the senator was.''

''Wasn't there a big budget vote last Friday?'' Larry asked. ''Wouldn't most of the congressmen have been in D.C.? The paper ought to have a record of who voted and who was absent.''

''I could call the *Journal-Constitution*'s Washington bureau and see who covered the vote," Jenny Lee offered. "We want to know if Rawlings was on the Senate floor, right?"

"And Downs," Amanda reminded her. "See if he was there for the vote in the House."

"That won't eliminate any members of their staffs from suspicion," Donelli pointed out.

"I guess we'll need travel records for that," Amanda agreed, casting a look at Joe, who responded with a familiar sigh of resignation.

"I know. I know. I'll go lock myself away with my computer and see what I can find on these folks and on Ms. LaPalma."

"Can I help?" Pete asked, immediately on his feet to follow. "I want to see what you do."

"Somehow the thought of you knowing how to do computerized research into stuff like this strikes terror into my heart," Donelli retorted to Pete's obvious dismay. He grinned and relented. "At least it's all nice and legal, public information. I suppose it's better than turning you loose to con tourists again."

When they'd left the room, Larry looked at Amanda. "What was that all about?"

"You don't want to know," she assured him. "Why don't you all quit for the night? Maybe you can get to more of the rental agencies tomorrow. And maybe those other two body shops will be open."

"I'll just make that call to the paper first," Jenny Lee

said, going to the phone on the wall. It took her three calls to track down the right reporter. Finally she hung up with a sigh. "A dead end. Both Downs and Rawlings were there for the votes. The reporter even remembers seeing Fine on the floor with Rawlings at one point. I asked about other staffers. He said the only other one he remembers seeing was—and I quote—'the cute blond chick.' "

"Valerie LaPalma," Amanda guessed, not bothering to comment on the reporter's sexist remark. She was too tired for a feminist diatribe, and she'd be preaching to the converts anyway. That reporter wasn't even within shouting distance.

"What time was the vote?" she asked instead.

"About eight o'clock in the House," Jenny Lee said, checking her notes. "Nearly three A.M. Saturday in the Senate."

"That would still leave time for any one of them to get here before the time of the accident, right?" Larry asked. "Didn't Mary Allison die about four in the afternoon on Saturday?"

Amanda nodded. She felt as if she were slogging through quicksand, getting nowhere and with her head barely aboveground. "Look, you two, you might as well go on. I'm so tired I can't even think straight."

"But I know you. You won't go to bed. You'll keep at it. Are you sure I can't help?" Jenny Lee asked, clearly worried that she might be left out of the good stuff.

"Not with this. I'm going to call my favorite international arms merchant and see if I can sweet-talk some information out of him."

Jenny Lee regarded her with concern. "Just be careful about what he wants from you in return."

CHAPTER

Sixteen

WHEN Amanda went looking for Donelli in his office, she found him sound asleep, sprawled on the sofa. Pete, however, was wide awake in front of the computer. Amanda wondered how that had happened, especially since it didn't appear that Pete was playing games.

"What's the deal?" she asked him, gesturing toward Joe.

"He was out in the fields about five-thirty this morning. When a guy gets to be his age, he needs his rest."

Amanda could just imagine how Donelli would react to that observation. "Does he know you're messing around on the computer?"

"Who's messing around?" Pete asked indignantly. "He showed me what he was doing. I've got all the access codes for the computer banks right here. See?" He waved them under her nose. "I'm just following up a little."

"Oh?" she said skeptically.

"For instance, this Valerie dame seems to have a slight cash flow problem. She's got a mess of credit cards, and they're all maxed out. She's behind on her mortgage, too."

Amanda had to admit she was impressed. "And you found all this on your own?"

"More or less. Once you know how to access this kind of stuff, it's a breeze. Joe's tapped into lots of computer banks and stuff. I've been through all that. The printouts are over there."

"If you've done all that, what are you up to now?"

"I'm working on breaking the code to her bank records, but so far no luck."

Amanda closed her eyes, trying to imagine Pete in prison garb. Unfortunately the picture was very clear. "Maybe that's just as well," she told him. "I'd hate to watch them cart you off to jail for illegal hacking."

Pete looked disappointed. "You want me to stop?"

"For now I think you ought to stick to what's legally available. You've been a terrific help, but you need some rest, too. Tomorrow's one of the busiest days of the week out at that stand."

"I thought I'd work with you tomorrow," he protested.

"That stand's your job, isn't it?"

"I guess," he grumbled.

"You don't back out of a responsibility just because something more interesting comes along. There will be plenty of work you can help with after you shut that stand down for the day. Okay?"

"I suppose."

"Off to bed, young man."

Shoulders slumped dejectedly, he headed for the door. Amanda sensed that he needed something, some reassurance, perhaps, that he was becoming a vital part of the family as well as of the investigation. It was all too easy for her to forget that for all his grown-up ways, Pete was still just a boy, barely into his teens. From what little she knew, he was also a boy in desperate need of acceptance.

Inexperienced in meeting such a need and flying by the seat of her pants, Amanda called out, "Hey, Pete."

He stopped, but he didn't turn around. "Yeah."

"I'm really glad you're here. It felt a lot better when I was gone knowing that you were around to help Joe keep an eye on things. He works awfully hard, too hard, if someone's not here to make him take time off."

Pete's expression was filled with skepticism. "You really think me being here makes a difference?"

There was no mistaking the wistfulness in his voice. She smiled at him. "Really."

For an instant it looked as if he might run back and hug her. Amanda held her breath, praying that he would. Finally, though, he opted for a thumbs-up sign.

"You guys are pretty okay, too," he muttered in a voice so low, it was almost as if he were afraid to make the admission aloud. Still, there was a new spring in his step this time when he left for bed.

After he'd gone, Amanda sat for a long time staring after him and wondering what sort of life he'd had before he'd run away from home. Were his parents searching for him? If they were, there was no record of it in Atlanta. Jim Harrison had discreetly looked into that much for them. She and Joe had discussed the wisdom of checking the national missing persons hot lines for runaways to get a lead on his family. Did they have the right to keep his whereabouts secret? With every day that passed, they both grew more troubled by the ethics of it.

At the same time, their relationship with Pete was so fragile and his need for some stability was so apparent that they feared what would happen if he felt they'd betrayed him. It was already clear that he knew how to vanish without a trace when it suited him.

She sighed at the complexity of the situation they'd gotten themselves into just by wanting to help this wonderful, precocious, lonely boy. Something about his tough, independent streak had touched her from the first.

As she sighed, she heard Joe shift positions on the sofa. Glancing over, she saw that his eyes were open and that his gaze was fixed on her. Judging from his expression, he had picked up on her troubled thoughts.

"What's on your mind?" he asked, proving how easily he tapped into her moods. "Something about the story?"

"No. Pete," she admitted. "How long can we let things go on like this?"

Joe moaned and sat up, running a hand through his rumpled dark hair. He gestured for her to join him. When she was settled with her back against his chest, his arms around her, he said, "Not much longer, I think. There's not a day goes by that I don't wonder about his family and what they must be going through.''

''But what will he do if we tell him we're going to have to notify his family where he is?''

''That depends.''

Amanda heard the note of caution in his voice. ''On?''

''On why we want to notify them. I've been thinking about this a lot the past couple of months.''

Amanda tensed, guessing what was on his mind and uncertain whether she was ready to deal with it. She knew, though, that they had to get it out into the open.

''You want to adopt him, don't you?'' she said finally. She could feel the movement in Joe's chest as he exhaled a sigh of relief that she'd put his desire into words. ''Do you think that's feasible?''

''We won't know until we find out about his background. I think if we tell him that's what we want, he may open up to us. Once we know what his situation really is, maybe we can make it work.''

''What if we can't? What if his family insists he come back?''

''What if he has no family at all?'' Joe countered, his tone somber. ''What if we're the only hope that boy has of ever having a normal family life?''

Amanda wasn't convinced that the life-style she and Joe maintained was exactly normal, with her chasing stories until all hours and him exhausted from nonstop hours in the fields. They caught their time together when they could. It was better now that they were married. At least they slept in the same bed, but the arrangement was hardly traditional.

"Having him here isn't so bad, is it?" Joe persisted.

"No. He's a great kid. And I love you for caring so much what happens to him."

"Is that a yes, then?"

She wanted to agree, but she had to admit the decision to make Pete a permanent part of their lives worried her. "We're just working out the kinks in our marriage," she reminded him. "Do you think this is the right time to make a decision like this?"

"I think that we both have enough love to share with one kid who's desperate for someone to tell him he matters. Besides, he moved in the day we got back from our honeymoon, if you can call a three-day weekend in the Florida Keys with Oscar calling every fifteen minutes about your next story a honeymoon. Pete's already part of the adjustment process."

"You're right, I suppose. And that three-day weekend was your doing. I wouldn't have had a next assignment if we'd taken a two-week trip like we planned the first time we were supposed to get married. You said you had to get back to your crops."

He turned her to face him. "Did I hear a note of censure in there? Let's deal with one issue at a time. We have to decide about Pete together, Amanda. It won't work if you have doubts. What exactly are you worried about?"

When she didn't reply at once, he sighed. "It's not Pete that's really troubling you, is it? It's the marriage."

She hated the fact that he'd zeroed in on it so easily. Did she send out vibes about how scared she was? Finally she gave a reluctant nod. "You and I have both been through lousy marriages in the past. We've had problems together. There was a long time when we thought those problems would keep us apart forever."

"But we've survived them, and our relationship is all the stronger for having weathered bad times," he reminded her. "We've got a lot more going for us than you give us credit for. We have love. We have commitment. And we have experience. We've learned from those past mistakes. We've overcome problems that could have ripped us apart. If you ask me, that adds up to a bond that's pretty damned strong."

"I want to believe that."

He kissed her then, convincingly. "You know, Amanda, sometimes I think we're going to be sitting out on the porch when we're both in our eighties and you're still going to be wondering if we've got what it takes to make it."

She grinned at him. "Must be all that journalistic skepticism."

"Must be."

Sooner or later, Amanda realized, she was going to have to take an extra leap of faith. It might as well be now. "Let me finish up this investigation. Then we'll talk to Pete."

Joe nodded, obviously pleased. "I love you, Mrs. Do-nelli."

"You'd better."

It was morning before Amanda got around to calling Armand LeConte. She'd awakened to an empty bed and sunlight streaming through the windows. After showering and pouring herself a cup of the fatally strong coffee Joe had brewed before heading out to harvest more corn or tomatoes or beans, maybe all three, she dragged the phone over to the kitchen table, pulled out her precious book of impossible-to-get phone numbers, and dialed Armand's highly secured Virginia estate.

"*Bonjour.*" It was a perky child's voice that greeted her.

"*Bonjour,* Noelle. This is Amanda Roberts. Have you taken over your father's business?"

The question was greeted with a giggle. "Papa says I am very . . . What is that word, Papa?"

Amanda could hear Armand's amused voice in the background. "Precocious, *ma petite*. Now let me have the phone. You run along and do your lessons."

When Armand picked up, Amanda chided him, "It's a holiday weekend. Why do you have that child doing her lessons?"

He laughed. "Because she is lazy. If I do not remind her a thousand times, she will not do them ever. She thinks she will get by on her great beauty and my fortune."

"Armand, she's only seven."

"It is never too young to set priorities, *ma chérie*. Now tell me, why do you call so early on this holiday weekend, if you too are not working?"

"Perhaps I just wanted to hear your seductive accent," she teased.

"Ah, I wish that were the case. But, alas, I know better. You prefer that polyglot of Brooklynese and southern. So, what can I really do for you?"

"I was wondering if Valerie is still at your château."

"She is," he responded without hesitation.

"Is she expected back in the States soon?"

"You wish to speak to her again? She very much enjoyed your visit. I am sure she would not mind a call. I could have your call patched through."

Amanda was surprised to hear that Valerie's response to her questioning had been so positive. "Perhaps I'll do that, but not today. You know, Armand, I sensed that she was very worried when I saw her. Do you think she has cause to be?"

"She would not be in France if I did not think that," he admitted.

The reply came more slowly than his earlier responses, triggering Amanda's imagination. "What kind of danger might she be in? Does she know something about Mary Allison's death, perhaps more than she admitted to me?"

"That is something you would do best to discuss with her."

The reply was Armand at his most frustratingly diplomatic. Amanda was struck by a sudden thought. Even though she knew Armand's reputation with women and had guessed that he himself might be close to Valerie, she wondered now why he wasn't with her if that were the case. And if the danger were so great, wouldn't Henri be over there looking out for her as he once had for Amanda?

"If she is in danger, why is she over there all alone?"

"Why would you think she is alone?"

"You're here. Henri is here."

"You think my resources are so limited, *ma chérie?*" There was a note of tolerant amusement behind the question.

"Of course not," she said impatiently. "I just assumed if she were important to you, you would take a more personal interest in her protection, as you did in mine."

"Obviously you have made something out of this theory. Would you please explain it to me?"

"Armand, did she come to you herself and ask for help?"

He drew in a sharp breath. "What is it you are hoping to discover, Amanda? Be direct."

That from a master of evasiveness, Amanda thought dryly. She debated which angle to try first and went for the personal question, which might irritate him but wouldn't trigger alarms. "Are the two of you involved?"

"You have asked that before. I did not answer then, nor will I now."

"I applaud your discretion. In this instance, however,

I have the impression it is not necessary. I keep having this feeling that perhaps you don't know her as well as I'd once assumed.''

"Is that important, *ma chérie?*"

"It is if it was Senator Rawlings who asked you to let Valerie hide out in France."

"He did not," he responded succinctly. "Are you sure you do not imagine conspiracies where none exist, *ma chérie?*"

That was an evasion if ever she'd heard one. "If there is no mystery, Armand, then tell me who asked you to let Valerie take up residence at your château."

"Perhaps it is nothing more than a vacation."

"And pigs fly," she retorted.

"Pardon?"

"Never mind."

"I must go, *ma chérie*. Noelle has apparently chosen to forgo her lessons in favor of a ride which I had expressly forbidden her from taking not fifteen minutes ago. She is outside trying to mount a new stallion, which has a reputation for throwing riders. The child is going to break her neck one of these days if she does not learn some caution."

Amanda heard the alarm in his voice and figured she might as well throw in one parting question. Perhaps, distracted as he was by his daughter's plight, he would respond honestly without thinking. She knew perfectly well that there were probably half a dozen well-trained employees to catch Noelle if she should start to topple.

"How well do you know Representative Downs?" she asked.

"As well as I know many members of Congress," he said enigmatically. *"Au revoir."*

Well, that was a big help, Amanda thought with disgust as she hung up. That could mean that he and Downs were intimately acquainted, just as he and Blaine Rawlings were. Or it could mean they'd met in passing and had no personal association.

One thing his response hadn't done was answer the question paramount in her mind this morning. Who the hell had maneuvered Valerie's sudden trip to Armand's secluded château in the French countryside? Though he hadn't actually admitted it, she was more convinced than ever that the idea hadn't been initiated by Armand himself.

And had whoever arranged for the trip done it to protect the congressional aide or to keep her out of the way until he was certain there would be no more unfortunate questions asked about Mary Allison Watkins's death?

CHAPTER

Seventeen

AMANDA sat at the kitchen table for some time, the phone still within easy reach as she debated her next move. Jenny Lee had the rental car and body shop angle covered. What Amanda knew she ought to be doing was pursuing those sexual harassment allegations. She still felt that—true or false—they held the key to everything. Or maybe she just wanted to believe they did, because the threat of exposure provided such a tidy and powerful motive for murder.

She pulled out the list of female staffers that she'd tucked away the day before and checked off Leslie Baldwin's name. Five more to go—Theresa McBride, Beverly Washington, Glenda Harding, Sue Ellen Bledsoe, and Rhoda Nathanson. She supposed she could at least attempt to reach them by phone. Taken by surprise, they might reveal almost as much as they would in person, even if she lost the advantage of getting a good look at their faces while they answered. She reassured herself that she'd conducted enough phone interviews in her time to be skilled at detecting nuances in a voice as readily as evasiveness in an expression.

The first three she tried weren't at home—McBride, Washington, and Harding. She didn't leave a message on their answering machines. No point in alerting them about her desire to question them, even though Greg Fine probably already had.

She finally lucked out with Sue Ellen Bledsoe.

"Oh, sure," she said when Amanda had identified herself. "Greg said you'd be calling. What can I do to help?"

"How well did you know Mary Allison?"

"We weren't friends outside the office, if that's what you mean. She didn't take to women friends."

"Oh?" Amanda said, thinking how everyone had portrayed Mary Allison and Valerie as being so close.

"Well, she really saw herself as part of the power structure, she and Valerie LaPalma," Sue Ellen said, answering Amanda's unasked question.

She went on, "I guess she figured most of us lowly clerks couldn't do her a bit of good. It's not that she wasn't nice and all, but she wasn't interested in being best buddies with somebody who couldn't help her get to the top." She sighed. "I shouldn't be saying all this, should I? I always talk too much. It's no wonder nobody'd ever put me in a job that required security clearance."

Amanda decided to skip responding to that. Personally, chatty people helped her out quite a bit. She didn't want

Sue Ellen to wise up now. "Tell me about the men in the office. How do you like working with them?"

"Oh, the senator's a real dream. He never yells, not even when somebody screws up. Maybe that's because Greg does enough screaming for any ten people. He's a real perfectionist. I guess that's good, though. I mean, what if he was the kind who let mistakes slip through that would make the senator look foolish?"

"Has Senator Rawlings ever said anything to you that you thought was a little too personal, anything that embarrassed you?"

"I was wondering when you'd get to that. Somebody told me what Mary Allison was planning to accuse him of. I couldn't believe it."

"Who told you?"

"Now let me think a minute. I heard it a few times, but I'm trying to think who told me first." She was silent for fully a minute. "I remember now. It was Ginny Gates."

Amanda didn't recognize the name. "Who is she?"

"She worked in the office a couple of years back. We still keep in touch."

"Was she fired?" Amanda asked, hoping this was the break she'd been looking for, an ex-employee with an ax to grind or perhaps one who'd been harassed herself and had left rather than fighting back. "Or did she leave abruptly?"

Sue Ellen laughed. "Oh, my, no indeed. Everybody in Senator Rawlings's office adored her. They couldn't believe it when she said she was leaving. The senator did everything he could to get her to stay, told her she was making a terrible mistake leaving, even if she was going to get a bigger salary and a lot of power and perks and stuff.''

''Where did she go?''

''She joined Representative Downs's campaign staff. She's his press secretary.''

Well, well, well, Amanda thought. Wasn't that interesting? One of Zack Downs's key campaign people was apparently using dirty campaign tactics to destroy one of his political rivals. And who would disbelieve a former member of Senator Rawlings's own staff if she hinted that sexual harassment had gone on in that office?

''Thanks, Sue Ellen. You've been a big help.''

''I sure hope I didn't say too much.''

''Absolutely not,'' Amanda reassured her.

It took her five minutes after she'd hung up to track down a number for Downs's campaign headquarters in Montgomery and another ten to discover that he was at a rally in Birmingham. She told the person at headquarters who she was and which magazine she represented.

''I need to speak to Ginny Gates as soon as possible for a story I'm working on,'' she said, hoping the prospect of a mention of the candidate's name would tempt her into calling back pronto. ''I'm working at home today. She can reach me here.'' She gave the suddenly solicitous young man on the phone her number.

"I'm sure she'll get back to you right away. I think I can catch her either at the hotel or on her cellular phone."

"Maybe you should give me those numbers, just in case we miss connections. Then I can get back to her myself later."

"Oh, sure," he said, and rattled them off without a second thought.

Amanda absolutely loved campaign volunteers. They were so willing and helpful. "Thanks so much. I'll tell her how helpful you've been."

She didn't wait for a return call but started dialing those numbers at once. It was the cellular phone that actually connected her to Ginny Gates, who sounded harried and as if she were standing behind the tuba in a marching band.

"What? What? I can't hear a word you're saying," she hollered over the music. "Just a minute."

Amanda could hear the sound of the music getting fainter. Finally Ginny heaved a sigh of relief. "There, that's better. I hate these damned portable johns, but at least I've got some privacy. Who is this?"

Amanda identified herself. "I understand you used to work for Senator Rawlings."

"Yes," she said tersely, her voice suddenly more cautious. "How'd you get this number?"

"From campaign headquarters. I left a message for you there, in case I didn't catch up with you."

"This is a bad time. Can't we do this later?"

"I'll make it fast," Amanda promised. "I spoke with someone earlier today who mentioned that you were aware of certain allegations Mary Allison Watkins was planning to make public about the senator.''

The statement was met by silence, then obvious suspicion. ''Who told you that?''

''It really doesn't matter. I was just hoping you could confirm that Mary Allison told you her plans herself.''

''Is this for attribution?''

''Yes.''

''Then I'm afraid I have no comment.''

''Why not?''

''Look, it wouldn't be appropriate for me to say anything about this. I'm working for Zack Downs now as his press secretary. I'm sure you can see the conflict.''

''I certainly can,'' Amanda said cheerfully. ''I was just wondering if you did.''

''Hey, wait a minute,'' Ginny Gates said, clearly taking offense at Amanda's implication of wrongdoing.

Amanda wanted her on the run. She kept pressing. ''Of course, if you were willing to explain how you knew what Mary Allison was planning or were willing to offer your own personal testimony that the allegations were true, then I suppose that would be a different story.''

''What are you getting at?''

''Just that right now this smacks of political dirty tricks. If you were the source of all those rumors and there was no substance to them, that would pretty much put you in the same league with the Watergate burglars, wouldn't it?'' Amanda suggested.

''Look, we need to talk, but not now. I'm in the middle

of this damned rally. It's a hundred degrees out here, and I've got hot, irritable media from the whole damned state waiting around to see Zack kick off his campaign with a rousing address.''

''I'm sure they can all manage just fine without you for a few more minutes.''

''That's what you think. The rousing address is still in my pocket. Zack's probably choking on his third slice of watermelon waiting for me to get back and save him. Look, I'll call you back in an hour, okay?''

''One hour,'' Amanda agreed, deliberately keeping her tone curt. ''After that, I start making calls to the networks and Associated Press.''

Apparently the threat worked, which it could only on someone who didn't know about Amanda's fierce competitive streak. It was fifty-seven minutes later when Ginny Gates called back. She sounded slightly less harried but no less uptight about Amanda's charges.

''I know what you're thinking,'' she said at once. ''But it's not true. I've never made those accusations publicly. If I had, don't you think they would have been front-page news by now?''

''You might have told people you knew would do the dirty work for you.''

''Then I must not know the right people,'' she countered. ''Again, the stories haven't made the news.''

Amanda decided she had a point, but she wasn't ready to concede that just yet. ''Okay, let's back up a minute. Did Senator Rawlings ever harass you on the job?''

"Never," she admitted with convincing vehemence.

"Do you know for a fact that he harassed Mary Allison? Did you witness it? Did she tell you herself?"

"No to all of those questions."

"Then what the hell were you doing spreading gossip like that to anyone, even with the most innocent intentions? You know better than anyone how explosive something like that can be, if it does leak out."

"Whoa, I said I wasn't certain the harassment had happened. I didn't say that I hadn't heard Mary Allison was going to say it had."

"But you hadn't heard this from her?"

"No."

"Then who told you?"

The question was greeted by the longest silence of their entire conversation. Just when Amanda was beginning to wonder if her source had suddenly clammed up, Ginny admitted, "Greg Fine told me."

"What?" Amanda was still astonished by how incestuous politics was. People went from staff to staff—hell, they went from political party to party—taking secrets and old loyalties with them.

"Look, Greg and I are close, okay? He was panicked about what was going on. He asked me how it should be handled if the shit hit the fan."

"Doesn't he have his own press secretary for that? Martin Oates?"

"Like I said, we're close. He knew he could trust me."

"But you turned right around and blabbed it," Amanda pointed out.

"To one person I knew would never tell," she said defensively.

Amanda didn't dare comment about the intelligence of anyone who thought Sue Ellen could be discreet. "Okay, you and Greg are close. I still don't understand why he thought he could trust you with this information and not Oates, whose first loyalty would obviously be to Senator Rawlings."

"I don't think he wanted Marty to get in an uproar over something that might not happen. I guess he also figured the fewer people in the office who knew, the better."

Amanda sighed. "One last thing. Was Greg worried because of the impact the charges might have on the campaign, or was he worried because he believed they might be true?"

Again Ginny hesitated, then admitted, "I think at that time he thought they might be true. I don't think he feels that way now, but then he was worried. Panicked, in fact."

"And when did you two have this conversation?"

"A week ago," she said. "No, more than that. It was Friday a week ago."

"The day before Mary Allison was killed," Amanda said, thinking out loud.

"Oh, Jesus. Oh, my God," Ginny whispered with obvious horror. "He didn't have anything to do with her death. He couldn't have."

Before Amanda could ask why she was so convinced of

his innocence or, perhaps even more important, why the possibility of his guilt had even entered her head in the first place, Ginny said, "I've got to go."

The phone clicked in Amanda's ear. It didn't take an intellectual genius to guess that Ginny Gates's next call was going to be to Greg Fine. Already dialing, Amanda wondered if there was any chance at all she could beat her to him.

CHAPTER
Eighteen

AN awful lot of what any reporter had to do was tedious phoning, boring searches for minutiae, and endless follow-up. Some of it, such as pinning a weasel like Greg Fine to the wall, was downright fun. For Amanda it almost ranked right up there with finally latching on to the thread that would unravel everything in some political corruption investigation. She had a feeling she was only one strand away from that key thread in this story right now, as she waited for Fine to answer the phone in his Atlanta apartment.

When he hadn't picked up after thirteen rings, she guessed he was already on the line with Ginny Gates and ignoring his call waiting signal. Not for one instant did she consider the possibility that he might not be home. In his position he would have an answering machine or a very efficient service to pick up in his absence.

He was not the kind of man who'd ever want to miss a call.

Since she'd already lost the element of surprise, she decided to head for town and try to catch up with him in person. Fine did not have a poker face. She'd be able to tell in an instant if he was panicked.

She didn't waste time changing clothes. She just snatched a linen blazer from the closet, added it to the jeans and T-shirt she'd put on earlier, then grabbed her purse, tape recorder, and car keys from the kitchen counter. She was all the way to her car when she remembered she hadn't left a note for Donelli. Rather than go back, she took the dirt road out along the edge of the fields until she saw his shirtless, sexy back amid the cornstalks. She tooted the horn.

"Let me guess," he said when he was beside the car, elbows resting on the window frame. "You got a hot tip and you're going to chase it down."

"That's why I love you. You know me so well."

"I guess that means I won't be coming back to the house to the aroma of peach pies baking in the oven."

"Excuse me. Are you forgetting to whom you're married?"

He grinned. "That could never happen. And you did bake last summer. I remember an entire freezer filled with pies and cobblers."

"A momentary aberration brought on by the absence of a man in my life. That's no longer a problem."

"Okay, so maybe I'll bake a pie. You going to be home to eat it?"

"I should be, but I'll call later and let you know my timetable."

His expression sobered. "Be careful, okay?"

"I always am." Just to prove it, she drove sedately all the way back to the driveway, then all the way out to the highway. Only when she was well out of sight of the farm did she floor the accelerator. She made it to downtown Atlanta in record time. It took her only a few minutes more to find Greg's high-rise apartment building just off Peachtree. It was convenient and uninspired, though the dogwoods on the surrounding grounds hinted of spectacular spring beauty.

In the building's glass-enclosed foyer, she buzzed his apartment, and again she got no answer. She went back to her car phone and called. He didn't answer. Nor did a machine pick up. A faint prickle of alarm crept up her spine. She went back into the foyer and looked for a buzzer for the manager. T. Hollings, apartment 106. Amanda pressed the button.

"Yes?" The voice was astonishingly frail to belong to someone given the responsibility of managing an apartment building.

"Mrs. Hollings?"

"Yes."

"This is Amanda Roberts from *Inside Atlanta*. Could I speak to you for a moment?"

There was the faint hesitation of a woman who'd learned

not to trust polite facades or legitimate-sounding identification. "You wait right there. I'll be out in a minute."

Given Amanda's inability to get through the secured inner door, she thought the order was unnecessary, but she waited dutifully.

The woman who appeared ten minutes later looked to be at least sixty-five, probably closer to seventy. Her hair had thinned and was tinted a striking shade of orange and frizzed into tight little curls. On closer look, Amanda realized those curls were held into place by bobby pins. She was wearing a housecoat in a flowered pattern that overwhelmed her petite body. But frail as she looked and sounded, her expression was fierce as she surveyed Amanda from head to toe, the security door firmly in place between them.

"What do you want?"

"You are the manager, T. Hollings?"

"Actually I'm his mother, but Theodore has gone to the market. What do you want?" she repeated as if she expected Amanda to pull a gun and turn into a homicidal maniac at any moment.

Amanda held up her business card where Mrs. Hollings could see it. "I was trying to get in touch with Greg Fine. He's not answering his phone or the buzzer to his apartment."

"Maybe he's not here."

"That's certainly possible, but I'm sure he would have his answering machine on if he weren't. Would it be possible for you to check on him?" Amanda hesitated, not sure she wanted to send this elderly woman off alone when she had no idea what she might discover. "I could come with you or we could wait for your son."

Mrs. Hollings took another lengthy survey of Amanda, then nodded and pressed the door release. "I think you're making too much of this, but I can see you're not going to let up about it until we've checked. I'll miss the whole ball game if we don't get this over with." She marched off toward the elevator, her high-priced sneakers making little squeaking sounds on the marble floor.

Not until they were in the elevator en route to the tenth floor did Amanda see that sweet little Mrs. Hollings was carrying a baseball bat hidden amid the folds of that oversize housedress. No wonder she'd been so intrepid. Amanda just prayed they weren't going to need it.

She decided it wasn't a good sign when they found Greg Fine's door sitting open by a crack. It was a worse sign yet when they tried to inch it open the rest of the way and it wouldn't budge. Amanda peeked inside to see what the problem was.

Greg Fine was sprawled facedown on the floor of the foyer, one hand outstretched toward the door. She couldn't see any blood, but he was awfully still.

"I think you'd better go call 911," she said, trying to keep her voice calm. Greg's own phone would be closer, but she wanted Mrs. Hollings away from there if someone was still lurking inside.

"Is he dead?" the intrepid little woman asked, trying to peer past Amanda.

"I don't know. Just go, please."

Mrs. Hollings looked doubtful. "You gonna be okay?" She held out the baseball bat. "Here, you keep this."

Amanda didn't argue with her. She liked the weight of the bat in her hands as she nudged open the door and slid inside. She knelt down beside Greg and tried to check for a pulse. It was there, faint but unmistakable. Amanda breathed a sigh of relief as his eyes fluttered open. He struggled for breath as perspiration beaded on his brow.

"You," he said, his voice weak but filled with venom. "Your fault."

Amanda was stunned by the bitterness of the attack, especially under these circumstances. "What's my fault?"

"Stirring everything up." Again he struggled to catch his breath. "Ruining it."

Before he could say more, the elevator doors opened and a team of paramedics led by Mrs. Hollings rushed down the hall. They had arrived with amazing speed. Amanda moved back out of their way, watching as they hooked up Greg Fine to oxygen and began the task of trying to save him.

Amanda was suddenly aware that inside his apartment the phone was ringing without letup. With everyone focused on Greg, no one paid a bit of attention when she went into the living room and picked it up.

"Mr. Fine's residence," she said.

"Who is this?" asked a nearly hysterical feminine voice. "Where is Greg? Is he okay?"

Amanda thought she recognized that voice. "Ginny?"

"Yes. Who is this? What's happened to Greg?"

"This is Amanda Roberts, Ginny." She tried to inject a soothing note into her voice to calm the other woman. "I just got here and found Greg in his front hallway. He'd collapsed, but the paramedics are here now. How did you know something was wrong?"

"I was talking to him, right after you and I hung up. He was yelling and all of a sudden he couldn't catch his breath. He said he had to call for help and hung up on me. I feel as if I've been calling back forever."

"That explains why his door was open and how the ambulance got here so quickly. He'd already called for one and had unlocked the door so they could get in."

"Dammit, is he okay?"

"Hold on. Let me see if I can find out anything." Amanda crossed the foyer and spoke to one of the paramedics. "Is there anything you can tell me about his condition?"

"Looks like his heart, but he's responding well. It may have been a false alarm, compounded with a panic attack. The doctors at the hospital will be able to tell you more."

"But he's going to be okay?"

"I don't hand out guarantees, but it looks that way to me."

Amanda went back and told Ginny what the paramedic had said. "Greg blamed me for this," she told her. "What had you said to him?"

"I asked him point-blank if he had killed Mary Allison because of what she had threatened to do. He asked me who I'd been talking to. Then he went into a rage," she said, choking back a sob that had never been far from the surface. "I never should have asked him that. How could I have even thought he would do something so terrible? I'm supposed to be in love with him."

Amanda hadn't guessed that the closeness Ginny had talked about earlier was actually intimacy. No wonder he had flipped out, and no wonder he blamed Amanda for ruining things. She wondered if he meant only his relationship with Ginny Gates or if his accusation included the destruction of the senator's campaign future.

She found out the answer to that on Monday. By then she knew from her constant checks at the hospital that Greg Fine was going to recover from what had turned out to be not a heart attack, but a serious warning that he needed to do something about the stress in his life.

Amanda was still trying to convince herself that she wasn't responsible for his illness, even indirectly, when Oscar called to say that Martin Oates, Senator Rawlings's media secretary, had called a press conference for four o'clock at his office. It was already after three. This time when she sped out of the driveway, she took the turn on two wheels, praying Donelli wasn't where he could hear the tires squeal.

She made it to Blaine Rawlings's office with seconds to spare. The television crews were up front, blocking the view, but she managed to squeeze through until she had a direct line of sight to the podium from which the senator was expected to make his announcement.

Martin Oates, Rawlings's handsome but weary-looking African-American press secretary, stepped to the microphone. "Everybody ready?" he asked, more to accommodate the television crews than anyone else. The print reporters had had their notebooks in hand and tape recorders primed for some time. At a signal from the CNN crew, he nodded. "Ladies and gentlemen, Georgia's distinguished senior senator, Blaine Rawlings."

The senator emerged from his office looking haggard. Not even his favorite bright red suspenders could counteract the impression of gray gloom that descended when he stepped up behind the podium. To Amanda's astonishment, Gregory Fine followed and stood to one side, his complexion every bit as ashen as the senator's. She worried that he was going to land back in the hospital, where he probably should have been anyway.

From where Amanda sat, this was a team on the run. She wondered exactly what the senator intended to talk about. Was he kicking off his campaign or ending it after all?

"Good of y'all to come out on a holiday like this," Rawlings said. His hands shook as he straightened the pages in front of him. "I'm going to read a statement first, and then y'all can ask whatever questions you like."

His glance swept the room, lingering when he caught sight of Amanda. He looked even wearier as he turned away to face the television cameras that were carrying the announcement live, apparently alerted ahead of time that this was to be no ordinary campaign statement.

"I've had a mighty fine run as your senator," he said.

Amanda began to guess where he was headed. She flipped on her recorder to get the rest on tape.

"I've been on the job nearly thirty years. I think we've done some good for this state. I hope we've done some good for this nation. But there comes a time in every political career when a man has to assess whether he can go on making the kind of contribution that means something. I've reached that point. Like the fading roses in my garden, I've reached the autumn of my career. It's time to let the younger folks take over and make the decisions that will affect their generation," he said, and for the first time his firm voice cracked with emotion.

He paused a minute, visibly gathering his composure. Behind him Martin Oates, Greg Fine, and other members of his staff were gazing at the ceiling as if they didn't dare to look at their boss for fear of breaking down. A muscle clenched in Fine's jaw, while Oates swallowed repeatedly, his Adam's apple working. To her astonishment, Amanda felt her own eyes becoming damp as she watched the senator struggle to finish what must have been the hardest statement of his long and distinguished political career.

Sticken by unfamiliar guilt, she wondered what role she had played in bringing him down and whether it would ultimately weigh on her conscience forever that she had done it with no evidence of any real wrongdoing.

"Traditionally, Labor Day weekend has been the official kick-off of the campaigning," he said finally. "I know it's a little late to be changing the ground rules for this next election, but I feel I can no longer delay my plans to retire." He looked for an instant as if there might have been more, but then he just gestured toward the reporters. "If y'all have any questions, I'll take a few."

The CNN reporter was on his feet at once. Because of his proximity, he was the first one given a nod by Oates.

"Why now, Senator? It'll turn this election into chaos. You're practically handing it to your opponent."

"I realize that, and it's not a decision I made lightly. You'll just have to take my word on that."

"Are you ill?" a reporter in the back of the room called out.

"The only thing making me sick is the way politics in this great country of ours has turned into a media circus," he said angrily.

Amanda thought it was an odd statement coming from a man who was taking advantage of the media at that very moment to get his message out. Unless, of course, the media he was referring to was actually only one intrepid reporter who'd gotten wind of his allegedly dirty laundry. Though Amanda continued to remain quiet, he, Fine, and Oates repeatedly cast wary glances in her direction as if just waiting for her to start asking questions about the harassment allegations. All she could think about, though, was why the senator had chosen not to fight. It nagged at her like a jagged fingernail.

The press conference went on long enough to cover his regrets during his tenure, his opinions on the most difficult tasks confronting Congress, and even a few light-hearted questions about how many prizes he hoped to win with his roses once he had time to tend them full-time. He responded graciously, a southern gentleman even in his untimely and obviously regretted retreat from public life. No one in the room, except Amanda, seemed to suspect that there was more to the story, at least not yet. Later, when they had time to hash out all the implications, they would begin to wonder and search for more detailed answers. In the meantime, Amanda wasn't about to do anything to alert them to what she knew.

When the press conference finally broke up, she edged her way to the front of the room. "Senator, I wonder if I might have a word with you privately?" she asked quietly.

He nodded curtly and led the way to his office. "I thought you'd be wanting something more than all that goddamned pap I delivered out there."

"Yes, I do. What's the real reason you're retiring, Senator?"

"Come on, gal, you can do better than that."

"Okay," she said, lifting her gaze to meet his. "Are you hoping to avoid a scandal?"

"What scandal would that be?"

He was toying with her, and they both knew it. To her astonishment, he seemed to be enjoying it.

"Let's start with the sexual harassment allegations."

He nodded slowly. "That's as good a place as any to start." He slammed his fist down on his desk. "They're a damned lie, and by God, you can quote me on that if you insist on going ahead with this story that'll be the ruination of my career.''

Amanda wasn't thrilled to have him lay a guilt trip on her. She was doing that well enough on her own, even though she firmly believed this whole sorry mess was not her doing. She was just trying to do a fair job of reporting it. "If they're a lie, why not stick it out and fight them?''

"Do you know how damned difficult it is to prove a negative like that?'' he inquired wearily. "Just by asking the question, you're raising the issue in a way that'll tar my reputation. Folks won't remember that no charges were ever filed. They won't remember that not one single woman on my staff ever accused me of a blessed thing.''

"Because the woman who intended to is dead,'' Amanda reminded him quietly.

"You say Mary Allison intended to file those charges. You've got a couple of hearsay confirmations that that's what she had on her mind, but you don't have one damned bit of corroboration, do you?''

His tone said there wasn't a chance in hell she'd ever find such corroboration. His certainty shook her.

"Not yet,'' Amanda admitted. She figured she owed him more. She owed it to him to tell him exactly what she was thinking. "I'm not even convinced myself that the allegations were true or that she intended to make them. But somebody believed it.''

His gaze narrowed. "What the hell's that supposed to mean?''

"I mean that Mary Allison Watkins did not commit suicide last weekend. I'll stake my career on that much. She might have died in a hit-and-run accident, but my guess is that somebody believed she was going to level those charges against you and forced her car off that road to keep her quiet."

He looked positively stunned. "Holy Jesus, gal, why haven't you said anything about that before now?"

"I don't have proof. Not yet, anyway. That's the story I'm going after, Senator. I've never been out to get you personally. I just want to know why Mary Allison Watkins really died."

He rocked back on his chair, his lips pursed, his expression thoughtful. "It seems the news of my retirement might have been a bit premature after all." He regarded Amanda evenly. "You expose whoever's responsible for the death of that pretty little thing, and I'll see to it you win one of them Pulitzer Prizes you reporters are always so hot to get."

Amanda couldn't help grinning, surprisingly delighted to see the return of his fighting spirit. "That's not quite how it works, but thanks for the offer."

She stood up and headed for the door, then turned back. "By the way, Senator, any idea who might have set you up?"

"Oh, I got a few notions who might be happy to see me out here fertilizing my gardens, instead of mucking around in policy on Capitol Hill."

"Care to share them with me?"

"I suppose you deserve that much for shootin' straight with me. Soon as I nail a few things down, I'll be in touch."

It was one of the oddest and most tenuous alliances of Amanda's entire career, but she had to admit she could hardly wait to hear what theories the senator came up with and whether they dovetailed with her own.

CHAPTER

Nineteen

T *UESDAY* morning, desperate for something to pull together the loose threads of her investigation, Amanda flew back to Washington. She left Jenny Lee pursuing the scant leads with body shops and car rental agencies, but more and more she was convinced that someone had driven their own car from Washington to kill Mary Allison. She wondered who kept time records for the senator's staff and whether those would reveal someone who'd taken off on Friday in order to make the trip. She figured Carla Boggs would be a good person to start with.

From there she decided to move on to a search of the parking garage for Senate employees. Surely, if the FBI could sort out the clues in the bombing of the World Trade Center in a few days, she could pinpoint a single, recently repaired car among those belonging to the Capitol Hill crowd. Maybe she'd even get lucky and there would be a record of parking permits for staffers that would indicate what kinds of cars they drove.

With her plan of action clear in her head, she strolled into Senator Rawlings's office and went straight to Mrs. Boggs's desk, ignoring Patricia Wilcox's condemning look. Obviously she blamed Amanda for her role in the senator's decision to quit. As for Mrs. Boggs, she barely spared Amanda a glance.

"You again?" she said in a tone that was abrupt but not unfriendly. "No way I'm fitting you into his schedule today. That man just got out of the hospital and he don't need the aggravation."

"Actually, it's you I came to see."

"My schedule's just as busy as his."

"There's one difference," Amanda reminded her. "You want me to catch whoever killed Mary Allison."

Carla Boggs seemed to weigh that for a minute, then nodded. "Talk fast. I ain't got all day."

"How would I find out who took off week before last on Friday?"

"I suppose I could get a look at the time sheets for you," she conceded.

It was more than Amanda had hoped for. "Thank you. I'm not looking for people on a scheduled vacation. I want the names of anyone who called in sick, took a half day of personal time at the last minute, that kind of thing."

"I'll have it for you, if you stop back around lunchtime. That's it?"

"No. Does somebody in the building keep records of parking permits for staffers?"

"Those go through parking services, unless you're talking about the senator, probably his chief of staff, and maybe Ms. LaPalma. They'd have spaces in the garage assigned by the rules committee. Parking services doesn't have a thing to do with that."

"Okay, what about everybody else?"

"You'd have to be asking a Mr. Dickson down in the parking office. It just so happens Mr. Dickson is married to my cousin. I'll give him a call, tell him you're stopping by."

When she'd made the call, she gave Amanda directions to SDG-61, between First and C streets. "Now you leave me to get some work done before Mr. Fine comes along and bites my head off. You can just imagine the mood he's in today with what happened down in Atlanta yesterday."

"I'll be back right around noon," Amanda promised.

"Twelve-fifteen," Mrs. Boggs corrected. "Not a minute later. I go to lunch right at twelve-thirty. I don't want to be missing my favorite show. That Victor's up to no good again on *The Young and the Restless*."

Walter Dickson was delighted to help out any friend of Mrs. Boggs's. He was tall and distinguished looking, with a touch of gray in his close-cropped, wiry black hair. He led Amanda into his office and gestured toward a chair.

"What is it you're looking for?"

Without going into her reasons, Amanda explained that she was wondering if any member of Senator Rawlings's staff owned a silver car. "I thought perhaps you'd keep some kind of identification on file."

"We do," he agreed. "Take it all down when we give out the parking permits. We get the model, the tag number, and put it all on computer. Spaces are assigned on a seniority basis, reserved spaces in the lots up close, unreserved way out."

"Terrific. I have a list of his staff, if that would help."

"It would, if I could do what you want, but I'm not so sure I should. I don't think folks would like my giving out private information to a reporter. Seems to me like there are rules against my divulging what's in our records."

"There is a public information act," Amanda reminded him, inventing the rest as she went along. "Your records are official government documents, right?"

His face creased with a frown. "I suppose."

"Then I'm entitled to see them."

"Don't you have to make some kind of formal request?"

She gave him what she hoped was her most persuasive smile. "I'm making that request to you. And Mrs. Boggs did tell you it would be okay, didn't she?"

Judging from his still worried expression, Mrs. Boggs wasn't turning out to be the magic weapon she'd hoped for.

"Why do you need this?" he asked. "Seems kinda

crazy coming all the way up here from Atlanta to snoop around in a bunch of parking lots.''

"It's a long shot," she admitted. "I'm hoping it will lead me to someone I need very badly to interview.''

His face set stubbornly. "Must be fifty people or more on that list of yours. I don't have time to be going through all those records, even if I thought it was the right thing to do.''

"You just told me they're computerized." She gestured toward the computer on his desk. "I could look them up myself. I wouldn't be in your way for more than an hour, maybe less. Please. If you have any doubts, call Mrs. Boggs back. She'll vouch that I'm trustworthy. And she knows how important it is that I figure out who was behind Mary Allison Watkins's death.''

His expression changed suddenly, softening in a way that spoke volumes. "This has something to do with that poor child running her car off the road?''

"It does.''

Though he still looked doubtful, Amanda could tell she had struck a nerve. Apparently he had liked Mary Allison and was as troubled by her death as Amanda and his cousin were. She sat back and waited while he pondered what to do. She was trusting that concern for Mary Allison would overcome his usual by-the-book scruples.

"You sure this will help?''

"I wouldn't be wasting your time or mine if I didn't.''

He nodded slowly. "Okay, then. I have to go check on

some equipment that broke down this morning,'' he said, standing up and moving toward the door. ''I don't suppose I can help what mischief you get into while I'm gone.''

''Thank you.''

He glanced back. ''Don't be thanking me. I don't know a thing about what you're doing in here. As far as I know, you're just sitting here waiting 'til I get back from looking into this emergency.''

Since he'd generously left her with his computer, Amanda prayed she could figure out how to get into the files. She sat down at his desk and studied the screen. He'd left the machine on. That was a good start. Hoping that he was the kind of person who only wanted to fiddle with technical things once a day, if that, she typed in ''permits'' at the prompt and pressed Enter. The machine informed her that she'd entered an inaccurate command.

Muttering under her breath, Amanda tried every way she could think of to access the files. She was about to curse her misfortune and leave, when she discovered the list of codes old Walter had taped on the side of the monitor. Bless his failing memory.

After that it was smooth sailing. She pulled up the permit records and began going through the names on her list. Because she wanted so badly for him to be implicated, she started with Gregory Fine, praying that he didn't have one of the spaces assigned by the rules committee. Apparently he didn't. She didn't want to guess what a blow that must have been to his ego, especially if every other chief of staff had one.

To her regret, it turned out that Fine drove a six-year-old blue sedan, an American-made compact. How very economical and politically correct of him.

She tried Valerie LaPalma next. Again, she wasn't one of the privileged few, fortunately. Her car fit her image—a flashy two-seater sports car, bright red.

Martin Oates had a serviceable minivan, listed as emerald green.

Just for the hell of it, she decided to check Mary Allison Watkins, wondering if that fancy new Jaguar of hers had been registered yet. She typed in her name. The computer came up empty. Had they already purged her out of there? Amanda couldn't imagine the government bureaucracy working that swiftly. Or had she had one of the precious garage spaces? She made a note to ask Walter Dickson about that when he returned, even though he'd probably be dismayed to discover her still in his office.

Thinking about Mary Allison's second car parked back in Mrs. Watkins's driveway, though, had aroused Amanda's curiosity. Would key staffers such as Fine and LaPalma, who traveled back to the home state with the senator regularly, keep cars in both cities? It would make more sense than renting each time, unless they made a deal with one of the rental agencies for special group rates. That was something else Mrs. Boggs could probably tell her.

Quickly Amanda ran through the other names on her employee roster. Only one was registered as owning a silver car, a 1990 Chevrolet. She jotted down the name,

Glenda Harding. She was also on the list Amanda had made of women she needed to interview about the sexual harassment allegations. She moved her name to the top of her list. She'd track her down this evening.

With Dickson still nowhere in sight, Amanda debated what to do next. While she was thinking, she idly typed Zack Downs's name into the computer, not really expecting it to show up.

When his file came up, she saw that he had permits for two different cars. Naturally. He was the type for conspicuous consumption. Unfortunately, the details about the car he kept in the main garage were hidden away in some rules committee file.

The other, apparently his concession to being politically correct, was a modest white Dodge Shadow convertible, one Amanda knew promised acceptably low gas mileage. Its assigned space was in a lot just a block away.

She couldn't stop thinking about that first car, though. What would be the primary vehicle of a man whose fiancée had driven a Jaguar? A Cadillac? A Mercedes? A Lincoln?

Perhaps she should try to get a look at the car in question. She glanced at her watch. She had a half hour before she was supposed to meet with Carla Boggs. Not enough time to make a run to the representative's home in Georgetown for a quick scan of his garage or the surrounding streets. Nor was it logical to consider surveying the congressional parking garage from top to bottom, hoping to stumble across his assigned space. It was not the sort of needle-in-a-haystack hunt she had time to pursue. She'd just have to wait.

Proud of her uncharacteristic display of patience, she gave up waiting for Walter Dickson and went in search of a copy of *The Washington Post*. She found a coffee shop where she could scan the A section to see if anyone else had been tipped to the brewing scandal in Georgia.

There wasn't a word about Mary Allison's death. Nor could she find more than a brief summary of Washington's reaction to the news of Senator Rawlings's impending retirement. Apparently the senator was keeping his decision to reenter the race under wraps for the moment. Thinking of Patricia Wilcox's reaction to her arrival that morning, Amanda guessed he hadn't even told his staff yet.

After reading through the *Post,* Amanda was able to cling to the possibility that she could still pull this story together and beat one of the best papers in the country to the punch, a rarity for a monthly magazine competing with daily publications. As competitive as she was, it was her favorite kind of journalistic coup.

At noon she headed back to Senator Rawlings's office, approaching the door at twelve-fifteen on the dot. Carla Boggs caught sight of her in the doorway and waved her back into the hall.

"I don't know what to make of this," she said, her expression indignant. "I went looking for those time sheets. Turned the place upside down. I still couldn't find them."

Amanda wasn't nearly as surprised by that as Mrs. Boggs was. "Who has access to them?"

"Just about everybody knows where they're filed away. Could have been anybody."

Thinking out loud, Amanda said, "But why not just take the one that was incriminating, if there was one, and substitute a corrected version? Nobody'd be the wiser."

"Maybe that's what they intended to do, but I got there first, before they could put everything back."

"So you don't have any information," Amanda said, not bothering to hide her disappointment.

Carla Boggs regarded her impatiently. "I didn't say that. I made a call and tracked down the originals in the payroll office. My brother's wife works down there. Asked her to make me a set of copies."

Amanda grinned at her, amazed by her network of relatives and by her resourcefulness. "And you found something, didn't you?"

"You'll have to figure that out," she said, pulling copies of two records out of her pocket.

Amanda looked at the names—Jonathan Lindsey, Mary Allison's clerk, and Valerie LaPalma. Lindsey had called in sick Friday morning, possibly because he'd known his boss was in Atlanta for a long weekend of wedding preparations. Or had there been another, more deadly reason? As for Valerie LaPalma, who'd taken three hours of personal leave in the afternoon, Amanda didn't know what to make of that. The *Constitution-Journal* reporter had sworn she'd been on the Senate floor later that night. The timing was all wrong for someone who'd headed for Atlanta to commit a murder on the following day.

"Well, do they help?"

"I'll know more after I talk to both of them," Amanda said evasively, not wanting to discourage her from further help. "Thanks for getting them for me."

It occurred to her that Gregory Fine might very well not have to do a time sheet, because of his position. "Was Mr. Fine in town all day last Friday?"

"He sure was. We had an important vote that night."

"Right. I remember reading about it. One last thing: Do most of the key staffers who go back and forth to Atlanta keep cars there, or does the office have a deal with a particular rental car company?"

"We lease the cars from a dealer down there for the senator, Mr. Fine, and Mr. Oates."

A dealer, not a rental agency, Amanda thought with a groan. That had never occurred to her. "Do you know which dealer?"

"Sure. I have to call 'em often enough for Mr. Fine. That man has himself a lemon. It was back in the shop just last week."

"Last week?" Amanda repeated, trying not to get her hopes up. "Do you know why?"

"He didn't say. Just asked me to call before he left here on Friday to make sure it would be ready for him."

"Which dealer?"

"Robinson Motors. Do you know it?"

"Very well," Amanda said.

Joseph Robinson was on the boards of half a dozen charity organizations in Atlanta. He frequently donated one of his Cadillacs for fund-raising purposes and offered a free car as a perk for the CEOs of the charities. Well aware of the promotional value of such contributions, he also had contracts with a couple of major sports celebrities who did his on-air spots. She wasn't surprised to discover that a man with that much PR savvy had ties to Senator Rawlings. The cynic in her wondered what kinds of favors he expected in return.

"Thanks. You've been terrific. I'll let you know what I find out about all this."

She went back to the coffee shop she'd just left and called Jenny Lee from the pay phone in back.

"Go by Robinson Motors and see if you can find out what kinds of repairs Greg Fine had done on his car last week. Check out the make and color, too. If it's silver and he had bodywork done, then go by his apartment building and take a look at it in person. Call Jim Harrison and have him meet you there."

"Where can I get you when I know something?"

Amanda gave her the number of the pay phone. "I'm going to grab a booth here in the back and wait."

"It could take a while," Jenny Lee warned.

Just then Amanda caught sight of Zack Downs coming through the door. "You have no idea how long I can make a cup of coffee and a sandwich last," she said. Especially now that she had this fascinating incentive.

C H A P T E R

Twenty

AMANDA debated making her presence known to Zack Downs, then decided to wait and see who turned up to meet him. Fortunately, as he found a vacant table and sat down, he wasn't paying any attention to anyone else in the place. His gaze was riveted on the door. Amanda was close enough to see him start nervously when an attractive young woman came in and headed his way. Something about the woman looked familiar. She suddenly realized it was the same woman she'd seen leaving his office a few days earlier after being loudly chastised. It looked as if she were in for a repeat battle.

But even though his jaw was set, his expression angry, Downs still stood and pulled out a chair for her. Old southern manners and good breeding died hard.

"Where the hell did you disappear to last night?" he asked, just heatedly enough that his voice carried to where Amanda sat listening intently.

"I told you I was going to come back via Atlanta," she retorted.

She was clearly less intimidated by his irritation this time than before. Amanda wondered what had happened to change the balance of power. If anything, Downs appeared even more infuriated, but he maintained a fairly tight rein on his temper.

"Why go to Atlanta, for God's sake?" he asked with that same hushed urgency. "With everything going on over there with Rawlings's people, you shouldn't be anywhere around."

"I had to see Greg," she said firmly.

Amanda guessed then that this was Ginny Gates, Greg Fine's girlfriend and Zack Downs's campaign press secretary. Amanda studied her more closely. She looked to be in her early thirties, older than Amanda had guessed her to be during their phone conversations. Dressed in a turquoise silk dress with a bright yellow jacket and a colorful scarf that pulled the whole ensemble together, she had a definite fashion flair for understated femininity. Her auburn hair was cut in a short, sassy style that flattered her big eyes and fine features. Right now those features were set in a belligerent glare.

"Okay, okay," Zack Downs said, clearly backing away from the fight brewing in her eyes. "Is he going to be all right?"

"He flew back with me this morning, against doctor's orders."

"What's he going to do now that Rawlings is quitting?"

"I don't think he's thought about it. He's still in shock. Frankly, so am I. I know that reporter was all over the sexual harassment allegations. I talked to her myself."

Downs looked thunderstruck. "You did? What the hell for? She's trouble, Ginny. Stay away from her."

"She caught me off guard at that rally on Saturday. Then I found her at Greg's not an hour later when I called back to see if he was okay after he'd hung up on me so abruptly."

Since she was clearly on everyone's mind, Amanda decided to join the two of them for a little tête-à-tête. Ginny clearly didn't recognize her when she pulled out a third chair at the table, but Zack Downs turned pale.

"I'd never want it said I eavesdropped on someone else's private conversation to get my information," she told them cheerfully. "How's the campaign going, Congressman? Or is the outcome certain enough that I should be calling you 'Senator'?"

"What the hell are you doing here?" Downs asked, just as Ginny said "Who is she?"

Amanda held out her hand and introduced herself. Now she had two pale people facing her.

"Isn't it enough that you ruined Senator Rawlings's career and sent his chief of staff to the hospital?" Downs asked.

"Did I do all that?" she inquired innocently. "How, when I have yet to print a single word?"

"You're like those media vultures who weren't satisfied until they brought down Gary Hart," he said.

"By exposing his tawdry little affairs," she reminded him. "He gave them the ammunition. In fact, he taunted them into exposing him. You can't blame a good reporter for doing his job."

Actually, she had to admit she was impressed with the congressman's righteous outrage. It was a nice act, considering how badly he'd probably wanted Senator Rawlings out of office. "By the way, if all of this is supposed to be my doing, I'm surprised you're not thanking me."

"Why would I do that?"

"I've just cleared the way for you to get a nice spot on the Foreign Relations Committee if you make it into the Senate this November."

Ginny gasped at the accusation. Downs looked furious. He turned to his press secretary. "I told you she was going to do this. I told you she wouldn't be satisfied until she destroyed me."

Amanda looked from one to the other, not sure she was following what he was saying. "Am I missing something here? I thought I was only guilty of destroying Senator Rawlings."

"Not you," he snapped.

"Who, then?"

It was Ginny Gates who answered, since the representative seemed incapable of speech. "Valerie LaPalma."

Amanda couldn't keep her mouth from gaping. When

she finally gathered her composure, she said, "How does she fit in?"

She already had some idea. It was Valerie, after all, who had tipped her that Downs wanted that Foreign Affairs Committee position.

When nobody answered, she took a wild stab at piecing it together. "Were you and Ms. LaPalma having an affair?" she asked Downs.

"Don't answer that," Ginny ordered. "She'll use it to crucify you."

Amanda lost patience. "I'm not out to crucify anybody who doesn't deserve it. I'm trying to find out who killed Mary Allison." She glared at Downs. "That should be your primary concern, too . . . unless you already know."

With his eyes closed, Downs rubbed his temples as if trying to massage away a nasty headache. Amanda could understand why he might have one. She rather hoped she'd given it to him.

"What do you want to know?" he asked, ignoring Ginny Gates's look of warning."

"Were you and Ms. LaPalma having an affair?"

"Yes," he said tersely.

"How long had it gone on?"

"It started before Mary Allison and I even met. We both knew it was only physical, at least I thought Valerie knew that. She seemed to think it would continue indefinitely, even after the wedding. When I told her it was going to end, she flew into a rage." He met Amanda's gaze. "I know I should have ended it long ago, but I couldn't seem to do it. Don't ask me why. Mary Allison was all I ever really wanted in a wife."

"Including in bed?" Amanda asked, expecting an explosion of outrage.

To her surprise, he didn't take offense at the question. Maybe he was just ready to start getting a few things off his chest, a form of confession, so to speak. Sometimes reporters learned even more about mortal sins than priests did.

"Even in bed," he retorted.

"Okay, so when did you tell Valerie it was all over?"

"The day before Mary Allison died. Valerie took some time off in the afternoon and we went to my place."

So that explained Valerie's leave time on that critical Friday, Amanda thought as Zack kept on talking.

"Like I said before, she went into a rage, but then she calmed down. She actually went back to work, but I was worried. I thought she needed to get away. I didn't want her telling Mary Allison."

"So you asked Armand LeConte to spirit her off to France."

He regarded her with astonishment. "How did you know that?"

"It doesn't matter. All you were trying to do was get her away from your fiancée, right?"

"Exactly."

"Is that what you told Armand?"

He shook his head. "I allowed him to think she might be in some danger. I knew that would arouse his gallantry. It would also assure that she would be surrounded by his bodyguards."

"So why was she still in town for the funeral? Why hadn't she left that weekend, maybe even that Friday night?"

"She did. She was in Paris by Saturday morning, I believe. When news of Mary Allison's death reached her on Sunday, she insisted on flying back for the funeral. When she realized that even though Mary Allison was dead I still didn't want her, she went back to France."

If what he said was true, then Valerie couldn't be a suspect in Mary Allison's murder, even though she had a motive for wanting her rival dead. Amanda made a note to call Armand and confirm the timing of those trips.

"Where were you Saturday before last?" she asked Downs.

"I was on the House floor for a critical vote until quite late."

"I heard the vote was taken at eight o'clock."

"There was other business to conduct. I left about midnight. After that I was at home asleep."

"Alone?"

"Yes."

So Zack Downs had no alibi for the time of Mary Allison's death. But Amanda wasn't sure he had a motive for wanting her dead, either.

"What kind of car do you drive?"

He seemed startled by the question. "A Shadow. Why?"

"Is that the only one you own?"

He shook his head. "No. I keep another car at home in Alabama. I bring it up once in a while."

"Where is it now?"

"In Alabama."

Just across the state line from Georgia, Amanda thought, her suspicions going into overdrive again. "Describe it for me."

He still looked puzzled. "It's a Mercedes."

"What color?"

"Silver."

Bingo, Amanda thought. So despite his protestations that Mary Allison was the woman he wanted, he could have been the killer. The past half hour could have been nothing more than a cleverly conceived charade.

But before she could get too elated at having Zack Downs as a suspect, perhaps joining Greg Fine high on the list, she heard the pay phone ringing. She jumped up. "Excuse me. That could be for me. I left this number with my office."

Both Downs and Ginny Gates looked relieved by her departure. She didn't blame them. She snatched up the pay phone on its fifth ring, just before somebody else made a grab for it.

"Amanda?"

"Yes, Jenny Lee. What did you find out?"

"Gregory Fine's car was in the shop all right. It had a damaged right front fender."

Amanda's heart started to pound. "Color?"

"Silver gray, just like we were looking for."

Of the two prospective suspects she'd netted in the past five minutes, Amanda liked Fine the best, especially with that damaged fender to add to the incriminating evidence. Even though she wasn't wild about his morals, she opted to put Downs on the back burner for the moment.

"Does Jim Harrison know?" she asked Jenny Lee.

"He's got technicians going over it right this minute."

"Can he get to the phone?"

"Sure. I've got one of those little cellular jobs. Larry gave it to me because he didn't like my riding around late at night without being able to call for help."

"Put him on."

"Looks like your hunch is paying off, Amanda," the detective told her. "As soon as I find out if this paint is a match, I'll turn all of this over to the sheriff and our friend at the FBI."

"You're going to willingly involve Jeffrey Dunne?" she asked, amazed by the idea, given their past history of territorial sparring.

"Since it's entirely possible that the sheriff deliberately let this slip through the cracks, I thought it wise to tip Dunne."

"I'm sure he'll be thrilled. Be sure to let him know I had a hand in it. That will really make his day."

"You'll get full credit," he promised.

"Will this be enough to make an arrest?"

"It'll be enough to haul Fine in for questioning. Then we'll have to put him behind the wheel at the time of the murder. That could be more difficult. Do you have any ideas on how we can accomplish that?"

"Not yet," she admitted. "But I will. I can promise you that." In fact, it would be her pleasure.

C H A P T E R

Twenty-one

AMANDA was still thoughtful as she rejoined Zack Downs and Ginny Gates. Apparently they guessed from her expression that the call had provided new information about her investigation into Mary Allison's death.

"News?" Zack asked.

Amanda studied his face to see if the question was spurred by a desperate need to know what had happened to his fiancée or by panic. Gazing into his eyes, she would have bet on concern.

"As a matter of fact, yes. I think we might have something that will prove that Mary Allison's car was forced off that road."

"You have proof of that?" Zack said, his voice tight. "What is it? Who in God's name would do something like that?"

Thinking about how fast Ginny Gates was likely to run

to Greg Fine with the news, Amanda shook her head. "I don't want to get into the details just yet. Let's just say I think we'll know for certain by the end of the day."

She wasn't the least bit surprised when Ginny shoved her chair back from the table and stood up. "I have to go."

"Where?" Zack asked. "We haven't even ordered lunch. I thought we were supposed to discuss next week-end's campaign swing."

"I'll get the schedule to you later. I have to get to another meeting," she said, shoving papers back into her briefcase.

Amanda made a split-second decision. She wanted to know exactly where Ginny was hurrying off to. "I have to go, too." She smiled at the other woman. "Why don't I walk back over to the Capitol with you, if that's where you're heading."

Ginny didn't appear pleased to have the company, but she was too savvy a media specialist to ever say a flat-out, insulting "no" to a reporter who might come in handy down the line. She shrugged. "Sure, why not."

They left Zack Downs to his thoughts as they hurried down the block. Ginny Gates set a brutal pace, but Amanda hadn't lived in New York for nothing. She had no difficulty at all keeping up.

As soon as they entered the Capitol, however, Ginny gave her a dismissive wave and made a quick turn. "See you. I have to make a detour by the ladies' room."

Amanda might have believed her if she hadn't been

heading in the wrong direction. As a matter of fact, she was going straight toward Senator Rawlings's office. Rather than chasing along behind, Amanda found a pay phone and called Carla Boggs.

"What now?" Greg Fine's secretary asked, sounding more amused than weary. "Who's doing this investigation, you or me?"

"I'd say we're just about even," Amanda conceded. "I'm looking for Ginny Gates. Is she in with Mr. Fine?"

"I haven't seen her in weeks," Mrs. Boggs said. "She doesn't stop by much, now that she's working for . . . Well, I'll be. Here she comes through the door right now. You want to talk to her?"

"Nope. Just wanted to see if my instincts were right. Thanks, Mrs. Boggs. I owe you one."

"More than that."

Amanda chuckled. "How about an entire dozen of the best cream-filled doughnuts in D.C.?"

"Once a week for a month," Mrs. Boggs bargained.

"You've got it."

After she'd hung up, Amanda tried to decide her next move. Assuming the police's lab work could prove Fine's car was at the scene of the accident, she had to find some way to put him in the driver's seat. So far she hadn't even been able to place him in Atlanta. Donelli was her best bet for doing that. He had great airline contacts who might be willing to look at their records for all Atlanta-bound flights on the Friday and Saturday in question.

The gods were with her. When she called the house, he

was actually inside taking a lunch break. "I know you're probably in the middle of things in the fields, but could you make those calls for me now?"

"You coming home when this investigation is wrapped up?"

"Yes."

"I'd say that's sufficient motivation. I'll make the calls. Check back with me in an hour or so. Are you positive you only want me to concentrate on Fine?"

"It's his car. I'm ninety percent certain of that now. He's the one I need to prove was in Atlanta on that Saturday afternoon."

"Okay, then. Talk to you soon."

Her next call was to Dee-Ann Watkins. Maybe she would recall something more specific about what had sent Mary Allison onto that particular highway on the afternoon she'd died. She found her at home, sounding even more despondent than she'd been right after the funeral. Maybe the reality of her daughter's death was finally setting in.

"I need to ask you a couple of questions about the day Mary Allison died," Amanda explained.

"You're still investigating, then?"

"Absolutely."

"I just wondered. When I didn't hear back from you, I thought maybe they'd convinced you, too."

"I'm sorry. I should have checked in, but I've been chasing leads. I don't want you to get your hopes too high, but I think we may have what we need to prove that Mary Allison didn't commit suicide."

"Oh, my," Dee-Ann Watkins said, her voice catching on a sob. When she could finally speak again, she said, "Thank you. Thank you so much. Tell me what happened."

"I'm still piecing it together. That's why I need to talk to you."

"Come on by, then. I haven't left the house in days."

"I'm in Washington, but I'll stop by as soon as I get back. I promise. Now can you think back to the day of the accident? Tell me exactly what Mary Allison had planned for the day."

"I've gone over this a thousand times in my head. We spent the whole morning together. Zack called and they talked for a while. Then she got on the phone with the florist. And then we went looking for her wedding dress. Right after she put the deposit down on that, we came back to the house."

"But she went out again. Where was she going?"

"I told you before, best as I can recall, she was just going for a drive to clear her head."

"She didn't mention any other errands? She didn't get a phone call or a message that she was to meet someone?"

"No. Of course, I wasn't in the room when she checked for any messages. I suppose someone could have called, but she never said that. I would have remembered before now. I'm sorry."

"That's okay. Can you look up the number for the record store where Lou-Ellen Kinsale works?"

When she had the number, Amanda called and went

through the same conversation with Lou-Ellen that she'd just had with Dee-Ann Watkins. Mary Allison's bridesmaid remembered no more than her mother had.

Even without any corroboration, Amanda was virtually convinced that someone had lured Mary Allison onto that highway. Maybe in his conversation with her that morning, Zack had suggested a rendezvous partway between Georgia and Alabama. Perhaps Greg had called and claimed that his car had broken down. Apparently everyone in the office was well aware of what a lemon it was. He could even have had a stranger make the call for him, adding to the credibility of his story. She liked that scenario better.

Amanda suddenly wondered what explanation Greg had given to the dealer for the damage to the car and how it had been brought in. Had it been drivable? It must have been, since he had clearly left the scene of the crime.

She called long distance information, then dialed Robinson Motors. Carla Boggs had told her that Greg had instructed her to call the dealership to see if the car was repaired. That was no indication of precisely when it had been taken it in in the first place.

When she got the body shop on the line, she said, "Hi. I'm calling from Washington. I was wondering if you were on duty when Mr. Fine's car was dropped off about ten days ago."

"That would have been Orville, who worked on the car. I'll get him for you."

"Ma'am?" Orville said politely a few minutes later. "Can I help you with something?"

"I'm trying to follow up on that accident of Mr. Fine's," she said, letting him decide if she represented an insurance company, the senator's office, or Mr. Fine personally. "Was the car in running condition when it came in?"

"Why, yes, ma'am, I believe it was. Of course, it came in on Saturday night, so I wasn't here to see to it personally. I just got a call on Monday morning, asking me to take care of it. It was already here on the lot."

"Thank you," she said, and hung up before he could start to wonder why she'd be asking a question like that.

Unfortunately, the conversation had been yet another dead end. Thoroughly frustrated, she called Donelli back. "Any luck?"

"Mr. Fine was not listed on one single flight from DCA to Atlanta."

Amanda clung to one last shred of hope. "How about Dulles? I know it wouldn't make sense for him to drive out there, but—"

"No," Joe said, cutting her off. "I checked that, too. Looks to me like he never left Washington."

"Well, damn," Amanda muttered.

There was a possibility she hadn't considered. She toyed with the idea that Ginny Gates might have been involved in the murder. Maybe her panicked reaction on the phone hadn't been fear that Greg had killed Mary Allison, but that he might be accused of a crime she had committed.

To make that scenario play out, Amanda needed a

motive. What if Ginny had been manufacturing claims that Mary Allison intended to charge the senator with harassment? And what if Mary Allison had discovered the dirty tricks campaign? Ginny might have borrowed her boyfriend's car and used it to eliminate the threat of exposure.

Unfortunately, a call to Zack Downs's campaign headquarters netted no solid information that could place Ginny Gates at the scene, either. She had been in Alabama, but no one could remember exactly when and where they'd seen her.

There was one way Amanda could find out for sure. She could go up to Greg Fine's office and ask both of them directly. One thing puzzled her, though. Ginny had said she and Greg had argued when she called his apartment after talking with Amanda. But had she been accusing him of murder? Or had he been accusing her?

As much as Amanda wanted to find some tidy solution that put Fine and/or Gates at the center of the plot, she couldn't find a scenario that made sense.

Which brought her back to the one other suspect who had a motive for wanting Mary Allison Watkins dead: Valerie LaPalma. Had she been in France at the time of Mary Allison's accident, as Zack Downs assumed?

Amanda called Armand LeConte. "When did you send Valerie LaPalma to your estate in France?" she asked after the usual flirting that came so automatically to the Frenchman.

"I believe I had the pilot take her on Saturday."

"After Downs asked you to see that she was out of the way for a while?"

"You have spoken with Representative Downs?" he inquired cautiously.

"At length," she reassured him. "What time on Saturday?"

"I believe it was around noon."

"Did the flight make any unscheduled stops?" she asked, grasping at straws.

"Where, for instance?"

"Atlanta."

"Not to my knowledge. I will call my pilot. You can hold on?"

"Absolutely."

Armand was back on the line in less than three minutes. It was amazing how quickly he could reach his minions when he needed to.

"Well?"

"He did land first in Atlanta. He said Ms. LaPalma had a business matter she needed to take care of. What is going on, *ma chérie?*"

"In a minute," Amanda promised. Her pulse was beginning to race, just as it always did when an investigation finally started coming together. "Did he say what time they finally took off?"

"It was close to six in the evening."

That just about clinched it. Valerie LaPalma had been

in Atlanta at the time of the accident. "Armand, can you patch me through to France?"

"I could, but it would be pointless. At her insistence, Valerie flew home this morning. She is in Washington. I believe, in fact, that she is back on the job."

C H A P T E R

Twenty-two

*E*VERY warning she had ever heard about charging off to accuse someone of a crime echoed through Amanda's head as she walked slowly to Senator Rawlings's office. She swore that she would not accuse anyone. She would only ask one last question, make sure that all the pieces fit, then she would turn what she knew over to Jim Harrison, Jeffrey Dunne, or any other law enforcement official who wanted to file the formal charges. She would still have her story. She didn't actually have to capture the murderer herself, for heaven's sake.

In the senator's suite, she found the door to Greg Fine's office firmly closed.

"Is he in a meeting?" she asked Carla Boggs.

"Ms. Gates is still in there with him."

"Would you ask if I can come in? Tell them it's urgent." Just in case Mrs. Boggs got a negative answer, Amanda went right ahead and opened the door.

Greg Fine hung up his phone and regarded her irritably. "I'm tired of you barging in here," he told her. "If you don't leave now, I'll notify security."

Amanda pulled up a chair and sat down. He reached for his phone.

"I don't think you'll want to do that, when you hear what I have to say," she said.

His hand stilled on the phone. "Okay. Make it fast."

"Were either of you in Atlanta the weekend of Mary Allison's accident?"

Both of them shook their heads.

Amanda looked at Greg. "How'd your car end up in the shop that weekend?"

He looked confused by the apparent shift in topic. "What does that have to do with anything? It was involved in a fender-bender. I'd loaned it to a friend."

"Valerie LaPalma," Amanda guessed.

He nodded. "But why . . . ? Oh, my God. Surely you're not saying what I think you're saying."

Greg Fine had turned out to be a lot quicker than she'd ever given him credit for being. "I'm saying that I think she used your car to force Mary Allison off that highway. Is she here? I'm told she got back to Washington this morning."

"I haven't seen her."

"I have," Ginny said, her expression suddenly petrified. She was already on her feet and striding to the door. "She was heading for Zack's office about twenty minutes ago."

Given what Zack Downs had told them about his breakup with Valerie and the one murder already committed as a result, Amanda could understand her panic.

"Now's the time to call security," she told Greg as she too took off running.

To his credit, he didn't ask questions. He was already dialing as Amanda and Ginny left the office. Then he was right behind them.

When they burst into Downs's office, startled staffers simply stared at them.

"Zack? Is he here?" Ginny demanded.

"No. He's still not back from lunch," his receptionist said. "Is something wrong?"

"What about Valerie LaPalma?" Amanda asked. "Has she been by?"

The receptionist began to look worried. "I told her he'd gone to lunch," she admitted. "She went looking for him."

"Call the coffee shop down the block and see if Zack's still there," Ginny ordered. "If he is, warn him to stay inside and tell him that Valerie's looking for him."

"But—"

"Just do it," Ginny snapped. "And when security gets here, send them after us."

Amanda was impressed at the way the press secretary had managed to keep her wits about her.

Outside the Capitol, everything seemed to happen at once. Ginny spotted Zack about to cross the street, just as Amanda saw a flashy red sports car speed out of a lot, heading in his direction. Valerie's car, she thought, recalling the records in the parking office computer.

She screamed a warning just as the car swerved. Zack looked up, caught sight of the car, and tried to dodge it, but not quite swiftly enough. As fear and understanding registered on his face, the car caught him behind the knees and tossed him into the air. He landed on the steamy pavement with a sickening thud. The car sped off, zigzagging through traffic, nearly hitting a group of pedestrians who'd just stepped into a crosswalk, then squealing around a corner on two wheels.

By the time Amanda, Greg, and Ginny reached Zack, it was clear that his injuries were relatively minor. He was sitting up, looking dazed but otherwise unharmed. He gingerly touched his legs where the car had struck and winced.

"What the hell happened?" he demanded.

"Looked like a hit-and-run," said a bystander.

Police descended from every direction, on foot and in cars. Half a dozen witnesses chimed in with their version of events.

Amanda flipped through the pages of her notebook until she found the description and tag number for Valerie's car.

"Officer, I think if you put out an APB on this car, you'll find a damaged front end."

"Who?" Zack said, then closed his eyes, his expression resigned. "Valerie, right? I saw the flash of red right before I went flying."

Amanda knelt down beside him to tell him the rest.

"Greg says he loaned her his car in Atlanta the Saturday Mary Allison was killed. Armand confirms that she was in Atlanta that afternoon. I think the police will be able to prove that Mary Allison didn't commit suicide that afternoon."

Amanda's words accomplished what even Mary Allison's funeral had not. Tears coursing down his face, Zack Downs buried his face in his hands. This time there was no mistaking the depth of his grief. As Ginny and Greg closed ranks around him, Amanda quietly slipped away.

Amanda stood in the shade of a centuries-old oak tree in Senator Blaine Rawlings's backyard while he announced to two hundred well-wishers that he had been persuaded that his decision to retire had been premature. He was reentering the race for senator of Georgia.

It was less than a week after police had caught Valerie LePalma trying to flee the country on a commercial flight to the Caribbean. She'd put up no struggle when they'd taken her into custody. Amanda had seen the pictures on TV. Wearing black and her trademark sunglasses, Valerie had looked almost relieved that it was all over. Someday soon Amanda knew she would have to ask Valerie if she had intentionally laid the groundwork for Amanda to discover the truth. For the moment, though, she was content to enjoy Senator Rawlings's exuberant return to the political arena.

He'd called the day before to invite her personally to the celebration. "Nobody deserves to be a part of this more than you," he'd told her. "You could have destroyed me with those damned sexual harassment rumors, but you kept them to yourself and stuck to looking for the truth."

"I was just doing my job."

"That's something we ought to talk about. I could find a spot on my staff for a smart, ethical go-getter like you."

Amanda had chuckled. "Trying to draw the enemy into your camp, huh?"

"I'm serious, gal. You'd be a damned fine addition to Washington."

"I'm a journalist, Senator. And my life's here in Atlanta, not in Washington."

"Hell's bells, don't you think my life is in Atlanta, too? That's what we got phones and planes for."

"Thank you for asking, but no."

"We'll talk about it tomorrow," he'd said, then hung up.

Amanda had told Joe about the offer.

"Aren't you even tempted?"

"Not in the slightest."

"How come? We could work it out, if it's something you want."

"Trying to get rid of me already?"

"Not a chance."

"Then my answer's final." She'd said it flatly and with no regrets. She wondered how long it would be, though, before the senator took one more crack at persuading her.

"Amanda?"

She turned to see Zack Downs regarding her with surprising uncertainty. "You're a long way from the Alabama campaign trail."

"I thought I owed it to Senator Rawlings to show up today and put to rest the rumors that I was after his job on the Foreign Relations Committee. We might have different ideas, and I might want my crack at that job someday, but I respect what he's done and I don't want to see him ousted before his time."

"Then the rumor was Valerie's doing?"

"That and those sexual harassment claims. She made it all up in some misguided attempt to help my career and to drive Mary Allison and me apart. When I found out, I considered resigning," he admitted.

"But you won't?"

"Senator Rawlings persuaded me not to. He said I'd already paid dearly enough for my sins and I had a lot left to give the country. I'm not so sure about that or about a lot of other things, but I'm damned well going to give it my best shot."

"Have you seen Valerie?"

He nodded. "She said she hadn't realized how much she loved me until I said it was over. I guess after that something inside her snapped." His expression turned pensive. "Funny thing about love, isn't it? It can be the most positive experience in our lives or it can destroy. Valerie is so staunchly independent she'll swear she doesn't need love, only to discover too late that we all need somebody to care about besides ourselves."

Amanda was still thinking about that when she drove

back to the farm later that afternoon. Just like Valerie LaPalma, she too had always thought of herself only in terms of her toughness and independence. Thank heavens she'd realized in time that that didn't mean she had to go through life alone.

For the first time in years, wrapping up her story wasn't the primary thing on her mind as she headed home. Tonight, all she wanted was to be in her husband's arms and make arrangements for Pete to be a permanent part of their lives.

Watch for the next

Amanda Roberts mystery,

DEADLY
OBSESSION,

Coming from
WARNER BOOKS
in May, 1995.

Chapter One

Post-partum depression. Some women got it after delivering babies. Journalist Amanda Roberts got it after turning in stories. The minute she had delivered her last exposé, she had begun to experience the let-down. She was starting to wonder if five minutes of euphoria over solving the puzzle was worth this awful *what-next* sensation that always occurred immediately afterward. The high didn't even last until the article was in print. At the same time, she had to contend with the worrisome glint of anticipation in the eyes of *Inside Atlanta* editor Oscar Cates, who was always thinking ahead to the magazine's next edition.

Just this morning Oscar had suggested that if

Amanda didn't come up with a fascinating story idea soon, he'd offer one of his own. She almost always hated Oscar's ideas. Since the November issue was coming up, he'd probably ship her off to some farm to do a feature on turkeys, or worse yet, to some socialite's home for a photo layout on setting a decorative Thanksgiving table in the Southern tradition.

In an act of desperation she began cleaning out files, hoping that some slip of paper would trigger an idea for her next investigative piece for the magazine. Unfortunately, she could spend weeks sorting through notes written on napkins and the backs of grocery store receipts without finding anything more exciting than a scribbled phone number for some no longer identifiable source.

She was reaching for her just-filled jar of gourmet jelly beans, hoping that maybe a burst of tangerine would put a little zest into her mood, when a shadow fell over her desk. Fortunately, it was a tall, lean shadow. Definitely not the ever-dieting Oscar, she decided. She dared a glance up.

"Ms. Roberts?"

She nodded, studying the man, who appeared to be in his midthirties and who was eyeing her jeans and T-shirt with a disapproving scowl. He had the look of a man intent on ferreting out Atlanta's worst-dressed professionals. Unfortunately, Amanda's designer-clad mother would have agreed with his quick assessment of her daughter. Amanda's casual but practical look would never make her a candidate for a fashion award.

Certainly this guy's attire would have withstood any designer's test. From his perfectly tailored grey suit, silk-blend shirt with monogramed cuffs and heavy gold cufflinks right down to his expensive, polished shoes, he was a testament to money and taste. Amanda couldn't imagine how people got through an entire day without a single scuff mark on their shoes. Maybe it required an attentive valet residing in the back of the limo. She glanced down at her own dull loafers and hurriedly tucked her feet out of sight under the desk. Since she couldn't crawl after them, she lifted her chin and met her visitor's gaze head on.

"Can I help you?" she asked politely, though she wasn't particularly inclined to be helpful to someone whose chiseled, aristocratic features betrayed such a haughty, supercilious attitude.

"I understand that you have quite a reputation as an investigative reporter," he said.

He made the observation with an expression of distaste that suggested he considered reporters only one step above pond scum on the evolutionary ladder. It also sounded as if he weren't personally acquainted with a single word she had written. If he'd hoped to flatter her, he was off to a bad start. Amanda was beginning to grind her teeth.

"So they say," she responded noncommittally.

He glanced pointedly at the chair beside her desk. "May I sit?"

"Be my guest."

When he was seated, his jacket neatly straightened and his cuffs precisely adjusted, he announced, "I am Hamilton Kenilworth."

He paused as if that were supposed to draw *ohhs* and *ahhs.* Amanda had never heard of him. She tried her best, however, to look as if she had and as if she were duly impressed. "I see."

"Of Kenilworth, Kenilworth, James and Donovan."

"Of course." She still didn't have a clue about who he was, but whenever names were strung together that way, she had to assume it was a law firm. She made a point of knowing as few lawyers as possible. She looked longingly at her jar of jelly beans, wishing she could politely scoop out a handful and find the soothing ice blue mint-flavored ones. She had a feeling this was not going to be a pleasant encounter.

"This is a rather delicate matter," Mr. Hamilton Kenilworth said eventually.

"I see," she said, though to be perfectly honest she didn't understand why this man had deigned to pay her a visit when it was evident he didn't consider her to be in his social or professional league.

"May I count on your discretion?" he asked, regarding her intently.

Discretion? The word sparked a certain amount

of hope. Maybe whatever he had to say would lead to something more exciting than a feature on turkey sightings or the making of little Pilgrim people from corn husks.

"Mr. Kenilworth, I suppose I am as discreet as the next person," she said. "But you must understand that generally people who come to me expect me to print something in a widely circulated regional magazine. Professionally speaking, I am not in the business of keeping secrets."

He colored a bit at that, an amazing reaction from someone she'd already decided was bloodless.

"Of course," he said. "It's just that this isn't something I'm in the habit of doing."

"You mean talking to a reporter," she guessed.

He drew himself up until he was sitting ramrod stiff. Some private school deportment teacher would have been proud of that posture. Amanda thought he looked downright uncomfortable. He also didn't seem inclined to elaborate. Amanda decided this had to be some kind of a diabolical test, perhaps dreamed up by Oscar to see how long it would be before she exploded impatiently and begged to do some lousy Thanksgiving feature. She figured—at the outside—it would take another five minutes of this awkward conversation.

His gaze met hers, then shifted away. "Actually, I meant baring my soul."

Clearly that explained why he didn't have much

knack for it, she decided. "To a stranger?" she asked.

"To anyone."

Now that Amanda could believe. Hamilton Kenilworth did not strike her as the sort of man who was actually in touch with his feelings, assuming he had any under that spit-and-polish exterior. She looked into his eyes, expecting to see little emotion in the cool, grey depths. Instead, his eyes were the slate grey of a stormy sea. Her level of interest increased another notch or two. She loved discovering seething passion under a calm exterior. It usually meant she was one step away from the heart of a story.

"Could I get you a cup of coffee?" she offered, hoping that would relax him so he'd spill his guts in a more timely fashion.

He shook his head. "No, really, I think it's best if I just get this over with. You see, it's about my child, Lauren. And my wife, of course," he added almost as an afterthought.

His gaze met Amanda's, and this time there was no mistaking the turmoil. "They're missing."

He said it with a bleak matter-of-factness that sent a chill down her spine. "Have you contacted the police?"

"No."

"Why not?"

"Believe me, I know how the police will regard this. You see it's not the first time Margaret has disappeared. She gets some crazy idea into her head and just takes off, dragging Lauren with her. In the past, though, she's always come back, just about the time she figures I'll be frantic. That's why the police won't take it seriously. They've seen what's happened on the previous occasions."

Amanda wondered whether she dared to suggest counseling. It seemed more appropriate than bringing his tale of marital woes to a reporter. The last thing she wanted to get involved in was some convoluted domestic dispute.

"Have you considered hiring a private detective?"

"I've had one working on the case for the past two weeks. He has come up with nothing, not a single trace. She hasn't turned up in any of the usual places. She's not with her family. She hasn't gone to our beach house in Hilton Head. Her best friend hasn't spoken with her in over three weeks. Frankly, I'm getting worried that something has happened this time. That's why I'm turning to you."

Amanda still wasn't entirely clear about where she fit into his plans and she was sure he had very definite plans in mind. His kind of pin-striped, button-down types always did. "I'm a reporter, Mr. Kenilworth. Not a detective. Where's the story?"

He regarded her with a wry expression. "Prominent attorney's wife flees with his daughter. What sort of scandal drove her away? Where is she hiding?" He dropped the tabloid tenor from his manner and said in a smug tone that was more in character, "I can't imagine that the questions wouldn't intrigue you."

Amanda was startled by what she thought he was suggesting. She wanted him to spell it out for her. "Let me get this straight. You want me to find your wife and daughter and out of this I get what?"

"A story that will sell magazines, of course. The Kenilworth name on the cover ought to do it."

To her regret, Amanda could definitely see the possibilities, especially if Kenilworth, Kenilworth, James and Donovan carried the kind of social clout he seemed to think it did. She wished she could slip away to confirm that with Oscar. She knew, however, that now was not a good time for an interruption.

She had to admit she was fascinated, if also a little outraged, by people who used their children as pawns in domestic quarrels. Certainly a story such as this would give her an opportunity to explore that issue, maybe talk to some psychologists about the impact on the young victims of such adult power struggles.

And right now, with a mysterious teenaged runaway living in her own home, she was already caught up in one dysfunctional family drama on a very personal level. Exploring the Kenilworths' troubles as she delved into Pete's background seemed like a way to weave the usually diverse threads of her life into a single strand for a change.

Still, she didn't much like Hamilton Kenilworth.

Something told her that Mrs. Kenilworth had been one smart cookie to get herself far away from the smug bastard. Gut instinct made her disinclined to help him in any way. For once in her life, she wasn't overcome by a need to meddle in other people's lives, even from a safe journalistic distance.

"Why would you want to air your family problems like this?" she asked. Somehow it just didn't fit with his uptight image.

"The more people I have looking for them, the sooner I will have my daughter back with me. And my wife, of course," he added, again almost as an afterthought.

Amanda's gut instincts also told her there was something more going on than what Hamilton Kenilworth was telling her. Something also told her she didn't want to know what it was.

"I'm sorry. I don't think so," she said finally. "I think you'd be better off leaving this in the hands of your detective."

He looked momentarily surprised, then more determined and grim faced than ever. "Just think about it," he urged. "Promise me you will take the night and think it over. It's possible, Ms. Roberts, that a child's future is at stake."

"Are you saying that your wife is an unfit mother?"

He avoided her scrutiny. "That would be something you'd have to explore, wouldn't it?"

"Mr. Kenilworth, I'm really not interested in sitting here playing word games with you," she snapped impatiently. "Is your child in some sort of danger or not?"

"If I tell you that she is, will you do the story?"

"No, I'll call the police."

He gave a nod of satisfaction. "Good. That is what I would expect you to say. As I anticipated, you'll do quite nicely."

Amanda bristled at the suggestion that he'd been testing her ethics in some way. "Mr. Kenilworth, you're not interviewing me to play nanny to your child. You're asking me to launch a full-scale investigation into her whereabouts, to dissect your family life for some clue that will lead me to her and to your wife. Are you aware that such scrutiny won't be pleasant and that when I'm finished all the messy details will be made public?"

"Ms. Roberts, I just want my child back," he said quietly. "I'll pay whatever personal price that requires. If my wife is embarrassed, well, then, she should have thought of that before leaving, shouldn't she?"

He reached in his pocket and pulled out a photograph. For several minutes, he studied it, then sighed and laid it on Amanda's desk, along with a business card. "I will expect your answer in the morning."

He stood then and walked away without a backward glance. Amanda glared after him. The lousy, self-satisfied son-of-a-bitch, she thought indignantly.

Finally, when she could stand it no longer, she picked up the snapshot. Grey eyes stared back at her from a cherubic face framed by a halo of golden curls. The child looked to be five, maybe six years old, and was obviously dressed for a special occasion in her elaborately smocked pale blue dress and patent leather shoes. Her far-too-serious expression struck a responsive chord deep inside Amanda. She immediately wanted to see smudges of dirt on the child's cheeks and laughter in those solemn eyes.

The killer, though, was the expression on the face of the man holding her in the photograph. The cool, distant demeanor that she'd found so irritating in Hamilton Kenilworth just now was the antithesis of the warmth and adoration on his face as he gazed at the daughter he held. She had pegged the lawyer as someone who loved only three things—money and power and position. Now, faced with the evidence in this one snapshot, Amanda was forced to revise her opinion. Hamilton Kenilworth also loved his daughter, maybe even above everything else.

"Well, hell," Amanda muttered at the discovery. She supposed she was going to investigate his story after all.

Exactly as the lawyer had guessed she would when he deliberately left that photograph on her desk, she realized irritably. She couldn't deny feeling manipulated. But she also couldn't deny the flare of excitement that overtook her every time she began to dig into a new story. Disconcerting, though, was the unexpected hint of dread that this time she wasn't going to like what she uncovered one little bit.